DEMAIN F

Short Sharp Shocks!

Book 0: Dirty Paws - Dean M. Drinkel
Book 1: Patient K - Barbie Wilde
Book 2: The Stranger & The Ribbon – Tim Dry
Book 3: Asylum Of Shadows – Stephanie Ellis
Book 4: Monster Beach – Ritchie Valentine Smith
Book 5: Beasties & Other Stories – Martin Richmond
Book 6: Every Moon Atrocious – Emile-Louis Tomas Jouvet
Book 7: A Monster Met – Liz Tuckwell
Book 8: The Intruders & Other Stories – Jason D. Brawn
Book 9: The Other – David Youngquist
Book 10: Symphony Of Blood – Leah Crowley
Book 11: Shattered – Anthony Watson
Book 12: The Devil's Portion – Benedict J. Jones
Book 13: Cinders Of A Blind Man Who Could See – Kev Harrison
Book 14: Dulce Et Decorum Est – Dan Howarth
Book 15: Blood, Bears & Dolls – Allison Weir
Book 16: The Forest Is Hungry – Chris Stanley
Book 17: The Town That Feared Dusk – Calvin Demmer
Book 18: Night Of The Rider – Alyson Faye
Book 19: Isidora's Pawn – Erik Hofstatter
Book 20: Plain – D.T. Griffith
Book 21: Supermassive Black Mass – Matthew Davis
Book 22: Whispers Of The Sea (& Other Stories) – L. R. Bonehill
Book 23: Magic – Eric Nash
Book 24: The Plague – R.J. Meldrum
Book 25: Candy Corn – Kevin M. Folliard
Book 26: The Elixir – Lee Allen Howard
Book 27: Breaking The Habit – Yolanda Sfetsos
Book 28: Forfeit Tissue – C. C. Adams

Book 29: Crown Of Thorns – Trevor Kennedy
Book 30: The Encampment / Blood Memory – Zachary Ashford
Book 31: Dreams Of Lake Drukka / Exhumation – Mike Thorn
Book 32: Apples / Snail Trails – Russell Smeaton
Book 33: An Invitation To Darkness – Hailey Piper
Book 34: The Necessary Evils & Sick Girl – Dan Weatherer
Book 35: The Couvade – Joe Koch
Book 36: The Camp Creeper & Other Stories – Dave Jeffery
Book 37: Flaying Sins – Ian Woodhead
Book 38: Hearts & Bones – Theresa Derwin
Book 39: The Unbeliever & The Intruder – Morgan K. Tanner
Book 40: The Coffin Walk – Richard Farren Barber
Book 41: The Straitjacket In The Woods – Kitty R. Kane
Book 42: Heart Of Stone – M. Brandon Robbins
Book 43: Bits – R.A. Busby
Book 44: Last Meal In Osaka & Other Stories – Gary Buller
Book 45: The One That Knows No Fear – Steve Stred
Book 46: The Birthday Girl & Other Stories – Christopher Beck
Book 47: Crowded House & Other Stories - S.J. Budd
Book 48: Hand To Mouth – Deborah Sheldon
Book 49: Moonlight Gunshot Mallet Flame / A Little Death – Alicia Hilton
Book 50: Dark Corners - David Charlesworth

Murder! Mystery! Mayhem!

Maggie Of My Heart – Alyson Faye
The Funeral Birds – Paula R.C. Readman
Cursed – Paul M. Feeney
The Bone Factory – Yolanda Sfetsos

Garland Cove – Deborah Sheldon
Death In The Dugout – Bruce Harris

Beats! Ballads! Blank Verse!
Book 1: Echoes From An Expired Earth – Allen Ashley
Book 2: Grave Goods – Cardinal Cox
Book 3: From Long Ago – Paul Woodward
Book 4: Laws Of Discord – William Clunie
Book 5: Fanged Dandelion – Eric LaRocca

Weird! Wonderful! Other Worlds
Book 1: The Raven King – Liz Tuckwell
Book 2: The Wired City – Yolanda Sfetsos

Horror Novels & Novellas
House Of Wrax – Raven Dane
And Blood Did Fall – Chad A. Clark
The Fallen – Anthony Watson
The Underclass – Dan Weatherer
Cheslyn Myre – Dan Weatherer
Greenbeard – John Travis
Tower Of Raven – Kevin M. Folliard
Welcome Home Natalie – Reyna Young
Little Bird – TR Hitchman
Society Place – Andrew David Barker
Axe – Terry Grimwood
Wicked Blood – E.C. Hanson
The Again-Walkers – Deborah Sheldon
Between The Teeth Of Charon – Grant Longstaff

Science Fiction Novels & Novellas
Odyssey Of The Black Turtle – Paul Woodward
Sons Of Sol – Kevin R. McNally

The 'A QUIET APOCALYPSE' Series
A Quiet Apocalypse – Dave Jeffery
Cathedral (A Quiet Apocalypse Book 2) – Dave Jeffery
The Samaritan (A Quiet Apocalypse Book 3) – Dave Jeffery
A Silent Dystopia (Stories Of A Quiet Apocalypse) – Edited by D.T. Griffith

General Fiction
Joe – Terry Grimwood
Finding Jericho – Dave Jeffery

Science Fiction Collections
Vistas – Chris Kelso

Horror Fiction Collections
Distant Frequencies – Frank Duffy
Where We Live – Tim Cooke
Night Voices – Paul Edwards & Frank Duffy
The Singing Sands & Other Stories – Rudolf Kremers

Anthologies
The Darkest Battlefield – Tales Of WW1/Horror

THE SINGING SANDS & OTHER STORIES

BY
RUDOLF KREMERS

© Demain 2022

COPYRIGHT INFORMATION

Entire contents copyright © 2022 Rudolf Kremers / Demain Publishing

Cover © 2022 Adrian Baldwin

First Published 2022

All rights reserved. No part of this publication may be reproduced, stored or transmitted in any form or by any means, electronic, mechanical, photocopying, recording, scanning or otherwise without written permission from the publisher. It is illegal to copy this book, post it to a website or distribute it by any other means without permission.

What follows is entirely a work of fiction. The names, characters and incidents portrayed in it are the work of the author's imagination. Any resemblance to actual persons, living or dead, events or localities is entirely co-incidental.

Rudolf Kremers asserts the moral right to be identified as the author of this work in its totality.

Designations used by companies to distinguish their products are often claimed as trademarks. All brand names and product names used in this book and on its cover are trade names, service marks, trademarks and registered trademarks of their respective owners. The publishers and the book are not associated with any product or vendor mentioned in this book. None of the companies within the book have endorsed the book.

For further information, please visit:
WEB: www.demainpublishing.com
TWITTER: @DemainPubUk
FACEBOOK: Demain Publishing
INSTAGRAM: demainpublishing

FOR MY FATHER

CONTENTS

THE SINGING SANDS	11
DEAR READER	57
THE BALLROOM UNDER THE LAKE	77
BIOGRAPHY	119
DEMAIN PUBLISHING	121

THE SINGING SANDS

Jean-Pierre sat cross-legged on the floor in the loft of my Amsterdam apartment. He occupied the space as elegantly as the beams of light falling through the aged, stained glass windows, like they had done for many years.

"The Dutch call them 'glass-in-lead' windows," he said. "I always thought that was a nice way to put it. Quite elegant really. Glass. In. Lead. That's exactly what it is."

Jean-Pierre leaned back lazily, stretched his arms over his head, and studied the windows he had just described. I was both happy and annoyed with his visit.

There had always been a strange duality about my relationship with Jean-Pierre. There were times when I was as fond of him as if he were my own flesh and blood — a brother perhaps, or a favourite nephew — even though we weren't related. I would observe his easy-going manner — his ability to charm and beguile men and women alike, irrespective of their race, religion, or class — and marvel at how *natural* it all seemed. There was just something about him, some quality that made him the kind of person one wants to spend time with, helped in no small manner by his ability to hold his own intellectually, in conversations about almost any subject, no matter how specialist in nature. There was always a tall tale he could share, or a fascinating tidbit of knowledge he could offer. His knowledge was frequently both arresting and surprising. He was a truly *worldly* man, as they say, with much to offer.

This was perhaps to be expected considering the top tier education both of us had received from a very young age (at great expense I might add), but I think it had as much (or more), to do with the fact that Jean-Pierre was an ardent globetrotter, frequently travelling to remote corners of the world, sometimes to countries which offered serious challenges to visitors.

He would tell people that his journeys were 'commercial expeditions', undertaken to supply mysterious, rich clients with ancient artefacts and esoteric antiques.

Rumour had it that some of the objects he sold were less than reputable, salacious even. To avoid scandal Jean-Pierre could be quite discreet about his work, so much so that his reluctance to go into too much detail actually planted the seeds of suspicion in some minds, suggesting that his were imaginary exploits; fantastical stories woven in an attempt to impress others. There was perhaps some truth to that — Jean-Pierre certainly knew how to embellish a tale — but despite the odd exaggeration I knew he was genuine in his pursuits, for he frequently brought me remarkable trinkets and ornaments. One could say I was one of his clients, as well as a friend.

Regardless of the occasional whisper, everybody seemed to be at ease with Jean-Pierre's way of life. His exceedingly rich family members were grateful that he had the good grace to stay clear of the day-to-day business affairs of their trade empire, I was grateful to have such an interesting friend bringing me delightful objects, and Jean-Pierre was grateful, well ... because he got to live the life he wanted to live.

But there were also times (I'm almost ashamed to say), when I resented him greatly. His bronzed and handsome features, toned by his many years on the road, seemed to give him an air of arrogance, as if he looked upon us regular folk as simple and unsophisticated beings. His practised conversational ease at times strayed into manipulative sophistry, easy to miss, but grating when one found oneself on the receiving end. His regular manner was warm and sincere, but he could suddenly pivot, and come across as cunning and calculating, as if everything he did and said was solely in service of a personal agenda; some coolly planned, selfish purpose.

Those were the times when I suspected that the real Jean-Pierre emerged; a person I hardly knew at all, despite our friendship having lasted over twenty years.

***

This time Jean-Pierre had brought me a silver tin, inscribed and engraved with ornate, somewhat imposing symbols and lettering. I studied it from all angles, holding it up in the coloured light, tracing my fingers over the writing and iconography.

"Arabic?" I asked.

"Yes, yes, but the tin isn't important. Open it, look inside," he said, his words underlined by a regal wave of his hand.

For some reason I smelled the tin before opening it. It exuded an exotic scent, hinting at unknown herbs, blackened silver, and sweat.

"Go on!" urged Jean-Pierre. I teased him by mock-examining the tin further, knocking on its lid, holding it to my ear as if listening to it — but eventually my curiosity outweighed my desire for mischief and I opened it.

The inside revealed a measure of sand, about a pint of the stuff, hued somewhere between a dark red and radiant ochre. I smiled, my heart beating with excitement.

"Oh ... this is good ... where's it from?"

"A patch of desert in Egypt. I found out about it when I visited Al-Eizam, a charming, ancient settlement near Mount Sinai. The locals call the place 'the Valley of Pain', and it's quite taboo, not meant to be explored ... But, you know me, I felt I had to smuggle out this sample at least."

"It's stunning," I said, genuinely impressed. "Not really seen this colour before ..."

I had been an avid collector of exotic sands from all around the world for many years now, something that Jean-Pierre was well aware of. So much so that I had turned it into a lucrative little business by producing ornate, limited edition hourglasses, filled with 'rare and unique sands', and selling them at a steep mark-up to rich people with a penchant for the exotic.

"Wait until I tell you what it *does*."

"What do you mean?"

"You're going to be impressed, I can assure you."

"Don't be a tease, tell me what this amazing sand can do!"

Jean-Pierre raised a hand, begging me to be patient, then stood up to retrieve a suitcase from the back of the loft. It was bulky and travel-worn, covered with stickers written in every conceivable language. There was something sweet about his desire to show off his travels.

"A demonstration!" Jean-Pierre announced, as he unclasped the patch-work lid. Inside the suitcase lay a reel-to reel tape player, accompanied by a stack of round tins. Jean-Pierre proceeded to plug in the awkward contraption, sifted through the tins, and retrieved the one he was looking for. I smiled at the theatricality of it all.

"You may have one guess!" announced Jean-Pierre, again raising his hand to ward off any of my questions. The player clicked into action, hissed and hummed for a bit as the initial empty length of tape disappeared inside, only to be taken up by the second spool.

"Well?" I asked, somewhat impatiently. Jean-Pierre just put a finger to his lips.

Then, a sound filled my loft unlike any I had heard. A low sonorous booming; modulating in an uncomfortable, eerie manner. It resonated in an almost aggressive way, making me feel like it existed not just as vibrations in the air, but that it had somehow invaded my skull, even my very thoughts.

But there was also another sound; playing a subtle duet with the louder overtones. This was a higher pitched, frantic sound. It evoked haunting loneliness, a melancholic quality of great poignancy.

"What on earth is this?"

"One guess!" repeated Jean-Pierre.

And then it hit me. I *knew* what this was. Jean-Pierre smiled as he saw the sudden recognition in my expression.

"Singing sands?" I asked, excitedly, already quite sure I was correct.

"The local Egyptians call it 'screaming sands', which is presumably why they're so afraid of it."

"Remarkable ... and you've seen this for yourself? Listened to it, in person?"

"Of course, you know me better that that surely? This is in fact my own recording. I can vouch for *the veracity of its origins* as they say. It wasn't easy to come by, mind you. I had guides to take me there, but they were so scared of the stuff that they gave me no more than thirty minutes to explore that ghastly place and record this sample. At least it allowed me to pocket some for my good friend Charles, eh?"

I was stunned. I had been aware of the phenomenon for some time now. There were rare places, generally in deserts or dunes in far-way countries, where at times the sands would sing. Marco Polo famously described his encounter with it as '*the sounds of all kinds of musical instruments, and also of drums and the clash of arms*' And I've seen enough other references to the phenomenon (in turn describing sands to be booming, screaming, laughing and whispering), to believe the stories to be genuine.

"What was it like? To be there I mean?"

Jean-Pierre pulled a face. "To be honest I don't wish to repeat the experience. It took some time for me to agitate the sand in just the right way for it to make the sound, but once it did it was overwhelming to the point of nausea. I nearly left. I was worried that I would faint, if you can believe that! But, I stuck with it and recorded about ten minutes worth. So there."

Retelling the experience caused a change to come over Jean-Pierre. He appeared confused and prickly, clumsy even, which is not something I had seen before with him.

"Are you alright?" I asked, genuinely concerned.

"I should go. Give me the tape. Keep the sand."

It was as brusque a dismissal as I had heard him utter. I was so surprised by this that I only managed to mouth the words 'thank you' after the door closed behind him.

***

I spent some time filtering the sand for any debris or contamination. This was a crucial test to determine if it was pure enough to be used inside an hourglass. Much to my delight there seemed to be no impurities to speak off.

Next I examined the sand under a microscope, to check its shape and consistency. Its red and ochre colour was even more impressive when magnified. The little kernels were perfectly shaped and of equal size. I was starting to believe this sand was absolutely perfect. On further inspection I noticed that the sand looked subtly different from regular sand, in a way that I couldn't quite define. It didn't seem to impact how it behaved, but maybe it offered a clue to its alleged sonorous properties.

Excitedly muttering to myself I searched my stock for an empty hourglass of suitable style and size, eventually settling for a gorgeous art-nouveau inspired piece. It was a special demonstration model with an easily removable top, so I could showcase different kinds of sand to clients. Once they made their choice I would produce the final version with artfully blown glass, airtight and seamless. My heart fluttering I filled it up.

Jean-Pierre's sand inhabited the hourglass as beautifully as any sample I had handled before. When I turned the hourglass over, the sand flowed wonderfully, catching the light with almost extravagant sparkle and flair. I placed the piece in the windowsill to enhance this effect and was blown away by the warm glow emanating from the glass and its content.

The light falling through the hourglass projected a shadow of the flowing sand on the floor, dancing, animated with magic and wonder. It was hard to look away.

I must have stood there for a while, staring in a mesmerised trance until all the sand had fallen through the funnel, and several minutes after. When I snapped out of my reverie I immediately turned it over again, unwilling to give up on this beguiling sensation.

Contemplating the origins of the sand, and still in awe of Jean-Pierre's tape, I listened carefully, hoping to pick up perhaps a faint trace of the alleged singing quality. I did not really expect to hear anything, understanding enough about the phenomenon to know that it would require a much larger quantity than this to produce that eerie song, but I was wrong: holding my ear close to the piece there was a hint of something ... an idea of a sound, a sensation as subtle as a feather falling to the ground. I concentrated deeply and held my breath, trying to define what I heard. Was it just my imagination, or was there really something in the air? The former was most likely, the latter would be a minor miracle.

Slowly, painstakingly, my ears managed to isolate a high pitched, gently modulating sound. There was a musicality to it, almost like a repeating melody. It reminded me of a faraway lament, or a soulful humming not unlike what can be heard in recordings of American spirituals. It was hard to put words to it, but it had an extraordinary impact on me. Bizarrely, the emanation somehow reduced me to tears, a raw sorrow gripping me by the throat, refusing to let go.

The effect was overpowering and not altogether unpleasant, but also brief — fading away when I failed to turn the glass over a final time. Nonetheless an aftertaste of deep, raw, melancholy lingered, until I decided to chase it away with a glass or two of Dutch 'Jenever' — the local equivalent of gin.

I did not admit this to myself, but I chose the vice of alcohol to keep me from returning to the hourglass and the disturbing sand it held — at least for the rest of the day — but I knew full well that I wouldn't be able to resist its call for long.

***

I was visited that night by vivid dreams, unfolding in a most peculiar way; I experienced a kind of lucid dreaming but had no control over events. (This was different from the lucid dreams I had experienced briefly when I was a teenager, when I was able to affect them in often delightful ways.)

The dream started with a stunningly beautiful vista; a sea of sand, undulating slowly, dunes rising and sinking like waves in a stormy ocean, foamy sand spraying in the gale. I knew, (as one knows things in dreams), that time itself was running amok, moving at abnormal speeds, going backward and forwards, in fact looping around to form a circle of events.

I wandered this environment aimlessly at first, but was soon drawn towards a booming, hypnotic sound coming from somewhere deep in the desert. The lucid part of me recognised it as the sound on Jean-Pierre's tape. I was excited to hear it again in what seemed to be its natural environment.

A higher pitched sound insinuated itself, cutting through the rumble. It beckoned me and I eagerly followed it onto a particularly high and treacherous dune. Wind whipped my clothes as I ascended, and I had to shield my eyes lest they filled with fine, red sand.

Once I reached the crest of the hill I could see as far as if it were a mountain. The Earth's curvature was readily represented in the horizon line.

One feature stood out; a dark structure in the far distance, fuzzy and indistinct due to atmospheric haze. It was the source of the insistent booming, even though I knew that no natural sound could reach this far.

I stepped forward, irresistibly drawn towards the structure, (was it a tower?), but the sand beneath my feet turned loose and treacherous. When I tried to steady myself I only managed to sink deeper and deeper as I struggled to escape its embrace. The high pitched sound was back, now gently modulating. There was a sad quality to it, as if it was mourning the loss of something.

My struggle was useless as the desert swallowed me whole. Sand covered my face, I closed my eyes and held my breath. I could still hear the booming — rhythmic, constant and implacable — coming from that faraway tower, or was it just the sound of my heart beating louder and louder, deprived of oxygen?

I tried not to breathe for the longest time until, eventually, I had to gasp for air. But my lungs didn't fill with sand, instead a fresh, perfumed atmosphere revived me. It was a cloying smell, of something sweet, something potent, a mixture of blood and flowers. There was a breeze, there were footsteps ...

I opened my eyes just as I awoke, and caught a glimpse of a city. It was the merest fleeting vista, teasing at me at the edge of visibility, but it was there long enough for me to be certain it was no mirage.

***

From that night onward I was lost. All I could think about was that dream city, the tower in the distance, the booming siren and the gentle high pitched emanation.

I went back to the hourglass to repeat my experiment of the day before. My initial resolve to ration the experience was completely broken, and I gave myself up to this desire without further restraint.

Each time the sand flowed I picked up a hint, an *echo* of that faraway place in the desert and its startling song. For days I indulged myself, barely pausing long enough to eat, let alone groom. But as incredible as the experience was, it would not and could not be enough; I needed more. I needed to hear Jean-Pierre's tape again.

This proved an elusive goal, at least initially. I rang many times, but he never picked up the phone. I went to see him at his house, but either he was absent, or declined to answer the door. I left a note, it was ignored. Meanwhile I kept returning to the hourglass, like an addict looking for a fix.

Each night I went to sleep hopeful to glimpse once more that mysterious city, and that beguiling towering structure, but even though I picked up flashes and snippets at times, it all started to fade away. I became desperate.

Jean-Pierre's strange evasive behaviour continued for a week, despite my evermore urgent efforts. I finally decided to stalk the bars and parties that he was known to frequent, hoping that he would show up. This approach finally led to success; I found Jean-Pierre around midnight in a brown cafe called 'Het Hert' (The Stag) in an old part of Amsterdam. I knew it well. It was a pleasant little place next to a pretty canal, not too busy, and often visited by writers, artists and eccentrics. Jean-Pierre sat at the back all by himself, nursing a Belgian beer. He nodded reluctantly when I asked if I could join him.

"I've been trying to find you," I said, puzzled at his obvious displeasure at seeing me.

"So you have."

"You don't seem very keen to see me," I said. I knew I sounded childishly peeved, but didn't care.

"Well … I would not quite put it like that," said Jean-Pierre, his tone softening.

"How would you put it then?"

"Disappointed I suppose."

"And why is that?"

"I knew you would come and find me, and why you would do so. I was hoping that I was wrong, but alas …"

"It's the tape …" I started.

"I sold the tape," stated Jean-Pierre bluntly.

"You did? There are no copies?"

A pained expression came over him then. "Look at you Charles. You've barely eaten in days, I can tell. You look ... gaunt." Then, under his voice; "*You need a bath*."

"You have to help me," I said, realising how desperate I sounded.

"Do I? Perhaps I've done too much already?"

I told him everything. The sounds, the visions, the dreaming ... I suddenly couldn't keep any of it to myself, the words spilling out of me like rats leaving a sinking ship. Halfway through my story I found myself clutching his hands without realising it, and withdrew them in shock. When I was done we were quiet for a bit. I ordered a beer, to give me time to compose my thoughts.

"I'm sorry, I genuinely am." Jean-Pierre said eventually.

"For what?"

"For lighting this fire inside of you. I'm afraid it will consume you whole."

"Come now, that's a bit melodramatic don't you think?"

He shrugged, as if it didn't matter what he thought. "What do you think I can do Charles? Like I said, I sold the tape."

"We can make a new one. We can go back to Egypt, to that place you mentioned. I'll pay for it all, it'll be a free trip for you!"

"No! I'm never going back to that place, do you understand?" snapped Jean-Pierre, leaning forward so that his face came close to mine. I was taken aback by the ferocity of his response.

"I didn't mean to ... Just ... tell me exactly where it is then. I'll go myself."

Jean-Pierre leaned back, looking defeated and tired. "I suppose there's no dissuading you from this foolishness?"

"None," I laughed.

"Then I will tell you all I know."

He produced a note-book from his bag, paged through it until he found the details of the travel arrangements he had made for his journey. I diligently copied all relevant data, thanking Jean-Pierre profusely, but couldn't avoid feeling a stab of dismay when I saw his grim expression as I did so.

***

It took me a week to organise the trip, paying a great deal of extra money to expedite swift issue of the correct visa and travel documents. I cared little for the expense, I would have paid anything to allow me to hear that song of the desert once more. Additionally, almost as an afterthought, I sent a small sample of the sand to a friend of mine for analysis. Erica was a lab assistant at the chemistry faculty of the U.V.A.; Amsterdam's biggest university. She would be able to reveal the exact composition of the sand.

Once I obtained the correct papers I managed to charter a semi-commercial flight to Cairo. It was a first time visit for me. Aided by Jean-Pierre's contacts I pre-arranged transport to Al-Eizam, the settlement near the evocatively named 'Valley of Pain' of which Jean-Pierre spoke. The whole trip took slightly less than one day. An oddly short time to travel somewhere that exotic.

I arrived at my destination in a ludicrous state of exhilarated near-exhaustion. My hotel was basic, yet stately and beautiful, a strange remnant of colonial times. The staff were extremely formal, so much so that I felt awkward even to speak to them. To make matters worse I tried to give the bell-hop a tip, a faux-pas which led to a look of such furious disgust that I almost considered changing hotels out of shame, but, it was late, and there likely wasn't anywhere better to stay.

It was fortuitous that I arrived in the evening, as I was forced to rest and recover before contemplating any trips into the desert. I decided to check out the hotel bar for a quick drink before turning in early. It was a bad call.

The only people there were local alcoholics drinking their shame away, and I soon gave up trying to start a conversation. I retired to my hotel room in a maudlin mood.

With some relief I fell into a deep slumber almost as soon as I lay down on the old, impeccably made bed.

I dreamed of ancient streets, glowing with a reddish aura, wisps of a mournful song drifted along boulevards and avenues, like an ethereal fog pregnant with faded memories. The streets, the buildings, they were all made of a kind of smooth, featureless stone, carved into slabs and bricks by means which I could not comprehend. But whenever I tried to focus on any detail, any sign of life or clues as to their provenance, my gaze *slid away*, unable to find purchase, as if this reality was too slippery to behold.

Amidst it all, I could feel, but not see, the presence of a towering structure, somewhere close by but never discovered inside the shifting realities of that dreamscape. Then, something beckoned me; a shape, the blurred after-image of a person, like a memory of an ancient dweller of this strange and majestic city. I followed it, towards the booming emanations that I had dreamed about before, but (with that inevitable logic of the dreamworld), I never got closer, no matter how far or fast I walked. I found myself running after my guide, at times chasing glimpses of other blurred figures. I desperately tried to find the tower; the source of the pervasive booming in the air, but found myself alone, chasing ghosts.

Success eluded me, until slowly the city streets themselves lost substance, and it all faded away.

When I woke, all I was left with was an aching desire to see that which was only hinted at in the tape, my dreams, and in the fragile visions produced by the sand in my hourglass.

***

The desk clerk, an officious little man with tattooed kohl under his eyes, was dubious about my mission to find the patch of sand described to me by Jean-Pierre. Several local guides were called in, much heated talk ensued. I showed them a sample of the sand itself, its dark red colour tinged with ochre hues sparked great debates for painfully long minutes.

Finally, they agreed to help me. After confirming the ungodly amount of pay I was willing to offer, we established some ground rules; I would be allowed to visit the forbidden Valley of Pain for one hour, enough to record sufficient audio for my needs.

There was great anxiety when I asked for a guide to accompany me onto the sands, and my request was refused, despite my protestations. They would bring me to the edge of the area but no further. As Jean-Pierre had mentioned, the particular patch of desert that produced the sand I was interested in was considered taboo, and no bribe was large enough to break it.

There were two guides (brothers, both confusingly called Mohammad) and three camels. I was told it would take us over an hour to get there, which didn't seem long to me. When I said so out loud I was assured in no uncertain terms that in the desert one could easily be overcome by heat, exhaustion, and other ambient challenges. Sandstorms, sand-blindness, snakes, scorpions ... there was no lack of potential danger. This struck me as fanciful but I gravely nodded my agreement, just to get the expedition going. Bar the tape recorder I travelled light.

The brothers' estimate proved off, but only by a little; it took us just over ninety minutes before they signalled that we were close. They pointed at a large ridge ahead of us. A collection of gnarly rocks stuck out from the sand at weird angles, as if they belonged to a giant's hand, clawing its way out of the depths.

The rock formation seemed incongruous to me, odd monoliths surrounded by nothing but wind and fine sand. Up close they proved much larger than I initially thought, large enough to offer plentiful shelter for the camels and the two brothers, who pointed excitingly at what lay beyond the ridge. I followed their gaze, and was confused for a moment. The desert beyond appeared much like the desert behind, or so I thought until my eyes stumbled upon an area of desert darker than the rest, demarcated by a border made of rocky debris. I recognised the colour immediately. Red and ochre, this was the place.

***

I tried to convince the brothers one more time to help me reach the sand. They reacted by angrily waving me on with hands weathered and leathered by the desert sun, chattering profusely. They took shelter in the shade thrown by the rocky monoliths, pointing emphatically at their watches. I admitted defeat, grabbed a leather case holding my portable tape recorder, donned a white cap to protect me from the glaring sun, and clumsily slid/walked down towards the red and ochre sands.

It was quiet. There was no breeze. I started to sweat, unaccustomed to such exertions, but the perspiration evaporated before it could settle on my skin. I scanned the ground for snakes and scorpions, but saw none, although at one point I saw two insects about the size of a fat grape locked in mortal combat. I chuckled to myself. Maybe the stories about the dangers of the desert weren't exaggerated after all, if one was a beetle.

As I approached my target the pristine desert sand was increasingly interrupted by rocks and boulders. Tufts of desert grass appeared. It became easier to walk, so I picked up the pace. When I arrived at the site I realised I had once again misjudged the size of rocks. The formations bordering the red and ochre sands stood as tall as me, some even taller. Not wanting to climb them I traced the perimeter until I found a passageway between two strangely rectangular formations. I stepped through, almost like entering a hidden alleyway. I could no longer see the brothers on the other side.

The ground stayed rocky for at least a few yards, until I reached the edge of the mysterious desert sand, where I paused, suddenly apprehensive. What was I doing here? Why did I care this much about some odd sand? I stood there for several minutes trying to convince myself that my actions were rational, and that there was nothing to fear. I did not quite succeed, but eventually stepped onto the sand.

Nothing happened. I took another step. I noticed a squeaking sound. Another step followed and the squeaking rose in pitch. It was almost a comical moment; each step produced a short-lived squeal. It was somewhat disappointing but still interesting enough to proceed. I climbed a reddish dune, squeaking all the way to the top. The vista before me reached further than I had expected, several kilometres at least, completely surrounded by rock formations whose neat boundary made them appear as if they were specifically designed to contain this rarest of materials. My eyes followed this boundary, until they found something: a black patch in the middle of the basin. I decided to investigate.

When I tried to descend the steep dune face I caused a little avalanche of sorts with each step, causing great heaps of the sand to roll down in waves. To my delight the squeaking took on a completely different character, transforming into a wistful high pitched modulating tone, soon followed by a deep booming expression. Finally! This was what I had come for.

I stepped up the pace, causing ever greater waves of sand to roll down. The singing of the sand rose in volume. The booming grew louder and more distinct. It may seem strange but I cried tears of happiness while I hastily unlocked the case holding the tape recorder. What a sight I must have made, clumsily descending great red sand dunes with a microphone, crying and laughing at the end of each recording, only to climb the next dune to repeat the process again.

    Finally I thought I had recorded enough material and took a moment to contemplate my next action; I knew I was supposed to make my way back to the guides, but my movements had taken me closer to the black patch in the desert. My curiosity took over and I approached. It appeared to be the base of an onyx tower. Was this a remnant of the towering structure I had encountered in my dreams? I had to find out.

***

What followed next was hard to understand, let alone put in words. Language can't convey with any exactitude that for which we have no concept to begin with. At best we I can try and approach a mood, a feeling. Glimpses and reflections, but not the thing itself. I know this sounds infuriatingly vague, but just like I could never understand the seasonal sense of being a tree, or the thoughts of a nocturnal predator, so I can never fully understand the sights and experiences of that day. But I will try.

Each step towards the black structure at the centre of this valley took me further away from my current reality. It was as if I existed inside one of my precious hourglasses, the sand flowing away from underneath my feet, dragging me down. I tried to run but my footsteps triggered a metamorphosis; a transmutation of time and space leading me somewhere incomprehensible, yet intimately known to me.

Sleek, majestic, stone walls rose proudly around me. Grand avenues and boulevards flowed between them with grace and purpose. The very air had changed — no longer hot and arid, but perfumed, fecund. I was in the city of my dreams, and its song was all around me.

Shapes floated through the streets. Human, yet otherworldly, but lacking in detail. I could not clearly see them. I wondered if they were connected to the high pitched song of the sand.

One shape approached me. A shimmering arm beckoned. It belonged to a faceless mirage, a beautiful apparition. It floated away and I followed.

I knew where it was headed. I could hear the booming tower drawing closer. With it came a sense of immense power. The air was thick with it, fizzing and crackling, exciting me in ways that were not proper, but impossible to resist.

My spirit guide did not take a direct route. We wandered the avenues and streets for hours, sometimes climbing steep stairs, other times going down impossibly long stone ramps. But I knew we were closing in on that structure, the tower, the source of the city's power.

We stopped in front of a gate in an arch. I knew what lay beyond it. When I made to enter the place beyond my guide halted me. Its oddly blurred, unreadable face closed in on mine until I felt something brush my ears with a delicate touch. Words were whispered.

They were instructions.

***

I awoke to a biting headache, disoriented and confused. My skin was cracked and blistered, my lips had burst like crushed grapes. I was too dehydrated to even moan. The brilliant glare of the sun blinded me totally, as I tried to make sense of where I was.

A shadow fell over me, offering respite. It was one of the guides, cursing and muttering, although I had no way of knowing what he was saying. He handed me a leather water skin which I accepted gratefully. Its contents were warm, but restored me somewhat at least. I looked around and found myself lying on top of a large, black, circular structure. It was the onyx base of the tower that I had sought in my dream, only cracked and weathered by thousands of years of exposure.

"My tape?" I croaked. A sudden panic took hold. After all that I had endured I couldn't bear having lost the recordings I had made.

The man looked puzzled. I had no idea if he understood me.

"Music box," I said stupidly, gesticulating wildly, as if that would help.

"Come," was all the man would say in reply.

"I need my tapes. I can't leave without them ..." I said weakly.

"Yes. Come."

I followed him, not knowing if he just offered some stock phrases he had memorised, or if he had really understood me. A glance at the man's watch told me I had been out there for less than an hour, including the time taken to record the tape. I had been unconscious for less than 30 minutes.

Afterwards, back in the hotel, I felt ill. A doctor was dispatched to see me; a pencil thin man, obviously alcoholic, but presumably competent. I was diagnosed with heatstroke and dehydration. When he asked how long I had lain in the sun he refused to believe me when I told him it was just a short while. My symptoms and sunburn were too severe for that.

I cared little for the prattling and poking, the tutting and murmuring. It was all background noise to me now, for I was given precise instructions. I was to revive the great city of the singing sands.

***

Back in Amsterdam I immediately set to work. Intense focus afflicted me like a tropical fever, allowing little else in my life. I drew detailed plans while listening to my hard-won tapes from Egypt.

The wonderful song of the desert conjured up images of the tower, the strange ethereal being I encountered. The city dweller's final whisper in my ear had been the kernel from which this amazing plan had grown. I worked like a man possessed to get it all down. My designs had to be meticulously calculated and thoroughly engineered, for what I needed had never been built before.

I took them to a raft of specialists: The glassblowers nearly dismissed me out of hand, until I made it known just how much I was willing to spend. The electrical engineers were more amenable to my unorthodox plans. They were a class of professionals who had seen and built all manner of innovative or revolutionary contraptions. They agreed it could be done, demanded a steep but fair price, and set to work. The carpenters worked without distraction.

I managed to enlist the director of an international trading company with strong ties to Egypt, to obtain the crucial final component for my plan to work. He mounted an expedition to Egypt solely staffed by his own personal workforce, bypassing the people of Al-Eizam completely. I paid him handsomely and provided him with additional funds for bribes and false papers.

Still, it took many weeks for my contraption to be built. There were setbacks: the glass housing was especially difficult to create, requiring new specialist instruments to be designed, just for this commission. The costs were exorbitant, nearly exhausting almost every financial resource available to me, but I no longer cared one whit for money other than it being a means to an end.

One day, about a week before my work would come to fruition, Jean-Pierre dropped in. His manner was gruff, brusque, bordering on rude. Not at all what I expected. Yet I picked up a whiff of despair, something was eating away at him, and I felt pity, or worry, or something akin to our old friendship stir in me. I invited him in.

I took him to my loft for coffee and jenever, hoping it would do him some good, but his eyes widened in shock when he saw the many detailed technical drawings now adorning the walls.

"This ... this shouldn't be ..." he stammered, walking from drawing to drawing, studying them with the intense glare of a maniac.

"I thought you would be impressed," I muttered, somewhat put off by his strange behaviour.

"Listen to me Charles. You can still walk away from this ... this madness."

"You don't even know what this is," I objected. "You might be surprised." I was disappointed and angry at myself, embarrassed at my need to feel validated.

"I know what you've *seen*," he hissed. "Anything to do with that ghastly city should be abandoned."

"You've seen it too?" I asked excitedly, wondering why that surprised me. "Then you know how immensely beautiful that city is. How wondrous and captivating."

"Forget about it. Now! Before it's too late," he shouted. Then, seeing my chagrin he babbled an apology. "It's my fault, I never should have given you the sand. Never should have let you hear the tape. I'm so sorry ... please ... forgive me!"

Something froze in me then. Once more was I reminded of Jean-Pierre's manipulative nature. I didn't believe him, despite the dramatic histrionics on offer.

"You'd better go," I said, brooking no further argument. "Your concern does you great honour but is completely out of place."

Seeing the resolve in my eyes Jean-Pierre visually deflated. His shoulder sagged, his eyes went dead. I shuffled him out of the house while he muttered pleas for forgiveness.

I did not know if he was seeking absolution for himself or for me.

***

A few days later, not long before I activated the device, Erica stopped by to share her compositional analysis of the sample of the sand I had given her just before my trip to Egypt. There was a jumpy excitement in her movements, her expression flustered. I suddenly realised just how attractive she was, but in a dispassionate distant way. There was no space in my head for sexual arousal.

I took her to my sitting room on the first floor, keeping her away from the drawings and designs hanging from the loft walls. She ignored the tea I made her and helped herself to a whiskey instead.

"Well Charles, I have to say this is a fun little mystery you've given me."

"How so?" I asked, wanting to get back to my device, but unable to suppress a hint of curiosity.

"Because the sand, well ... it shouldn't produce any sound whatsoever. And because its chemical composition is odd to say the least. But I'll get to that." It only took a few moments for her to empty her glass and pour another one.

"It most certainly can produce sound," I huffed. "I've seen it, heard it even, in the flesh."

Erica raised a hand, fending off my irritation. "I didn't say you were lying, just sharing what's odd about my findings."

"Tell me then, why should it not behave how it behaves?"

"There's more known about this phenomenon than you might think. It has been studied before you see?"

I nodded impatiently. "Yes?"

"Anyway, what is known is that the phenomenon only occurs when the sand kernels are pure, of a certain size, and are mostly composed of silicate."

"And my sample ... does not conform to that?"

"Well it does a bit. It's regular, the right size, but the chemical composition completely threw me for a loop."

"Oh, why is that then?" I asked, drawn in to her story now, despite myself. "Is this the mystery you mentioned?"

She smiled, excited to be able to discuss this with me. "Yes, it's gorgeous stuff, Red ... ochre ... pure, but I couldn't place it at all."

"But you solved it didn't you? I can tell."

Erica nodded emphatically, eager to share her findings. "Yes, I was stuck on the puzzle for a while, but then one day I was taking a stroll through the archaeology faculty, and it hit me ..."

"Go on," I laughed. Enough with the suspense.

"It was just a hunch, but I confirmed it soon after. The sand isn't really regular sand!"

"What is it then?"

"Fossilised bone. Ground, eroded, hammered by the years and the seasons and all that, but that's what it is." She grabbed my arm then. I was in too much of a shock to shake her off. "Charles it's a genuinely amazing find. Where did you get the stuff?"

***

The next day all the necessary final parts, components and supplies arrived, like a constellation of stars aligning themselves for a perfect ritual, a truly meaningful moment in time.

The workmen muttered among themselves as they laboured to put the disparate pieces together. They thought I didn't notice their furtive glances, their suspicious conversations, but I was well aware.

It was understandable; I had refused to tell them what they were building so they knew nothing of its real purpose. This had put their hackles up.

The device was being constructed in the dining room at the back of my house which I had emptied of almost all furniture and contents, for easy access. It was oddly touching to see it all fall into place. I felt like a modern version of a Nikola Tesla, or Charles Babbage. My work would surely change the world.

When the men had left, and the device stood finished, I stood in awe of its size and splendour. Despite having drawn up the plans myself I had been unprepared for its sheer grandeur.

Before me stood a gargantuan hourglass, reaching three meters tall, filled with barrels worth of red and ochre sand imported from the Valley of Pain. This is what I was told to build by the apparition in Egypt, to serve a glorious purpose. This is what would fulfil my wildest dreams, to revive the lost city of dreams.

It was held inside a most impressive feat of electrical engineering; an ingenious rotating framework, powered by a simple yet graceful brass hand crank. I was pleasantly surprised at the elegance of design that had been put into the crank itself; it was finished beautifully with delicate leaf patterns and intricate ridges to provide extra grip, while its spokes were subtly curved. I ran my fingers over its gently undulating surface to savour the workmanship. Somebody had enjoyed making this.

I briefly thought of Erica's strange findings, wondering what it meant, but ultimately decided that it didn't matter. The sand was what it was, and did what it was supposed to do.

I felt for a moment like one feels when standing on the edge of a sheer drop, when a sudden fear kicks in and one wonders: *One little step*, and it's all over ...

I laughed at my own morbid fancy, shook off the feeling of jumping to my doom, and pulled the hand crank. It rotated with a low rumble, like a bank vault closing, or perhaps a giant gate descending. Inside the contraption the hourglass started to move. Slowly at first, but soon with purpose and unstoppable force. So well made was the device that once it got going I hardly had to use any force to keep rotating it.

When the hourglass had turned nearly 180 degrees, and the sand inside started to flow into the lower compartment, it happened. There was no transition, no gentle fading in ... I just suddenly felt something stir, something fundamental was happening. Sound waves hit me like a gale in a storm — a physical force pushing against me, nearly toppling me over. The booming, the high pitched emanations, I was engulfed — much louder than I had ever heard it in my dreams. More pervasive, more real. I felt battered, accosted with a terrible insistence. I closed my eyes, trying to calm myself down, to give myself a chance to think, but when I opened them again the walls of my dining room had been replaced by the smooth, stone walls of the dream city. I smiled ecstatically, until I understood my grave error.

They set upon me almost instantly. The city's inhabitants were no longer blurred ethereal creatures, whispering secrets in my ears. They were corporeal, strong and malignant. I barely had time to take in their real appearance — their pallid mottled flesh, their hideous toothless mouths — before unnaturally warm, leathery hands grabbed my arms, my neck. A small crowd formed, and I was dragged along the street, stumbling and crying and begging for release. As if they would ever show any mercy, even if they could hear me.

They didn't parade me about for very long. After being dragged down a few alleys we arrived at a stately boulevard. There were more city dwellers here, observing my ordeal with expressions of glee and disdain. A particularly abhorrent creature — it must have stood at least seven feet tall — joined the proceedings, directing the rest to follow him. At this point I was beside myself with terror, and I tried to break away. All I managed to do was scrape my feet raw and bloody on the stone floor, having lost my shoes at the beginning of my struggle.

Soon, we passed through an archway of red stone (the same one I had seen before), leading to a coliseum. Inside, at the centre of it all, like a black star at the centre of a universe of pain, stood the towering structure that I had come to find; the source of the booming and screaming sand.

***

The thing stood on a large, round, onyx base — identical to the one I saw in the desert — towering over me, over the city, and the coliseum which housed it.

It was no ordinary structure. Like its base it was made of the deepest black material, hewn or constructed in ways that I could not begin to understand. There were impossible lines and angles to it, which my mind refused to unravel, as if it was a dirty thing to behold.

Sections of it moved; a mechanical breathing, a sense of hidden purpose inside. There was intelligence here, I could feel it.

The booming came from within the tower, and as I tried to make sense of what I was looking at I noticed it slowly, incrementally, rotated round its central axis. Whenever it moved the high pitched, modulating sound stopped. Whenever it stopped moving it started up again.

The walls of the coliseum were covered in strangely grotesque works of art; stone statues, depicting people of all ages, shapes and sexes, caught in poses of utter despair and pain. What manner of place was this?

Another rotation took place, revealing a great round object on the tower, about two-thirds of the way up. It reminded me of a glass orb or crystal ball, only it was the darkest of reds. It glowed (for lack of a better word) with an absence of light.

The rotation ended, and now I understood where the high pitched sound came from. The great eye, for that is what it was, focused on one of the human-shaped statues hanging from the coliseum walls. It came to life then, haltingly at first, then with increasingly jerking motions until it spasmed and twitched at ever increasing speed, turning it into a blur, not unlike the blurred denizens I had encountered on my previous visits in my dreams.

The unfortunate subject of the tower's gaze screamed. It was a raw pitiful sound, coming from a place beyond madness. It rose and fell in pitch and timbre in a manner which was almost impossible to bear, until the tower rotated once more, and its terrible eye sought another victim. It left behind a shape altered; a person clearly aged many years by the experience, now turned back into a statuesque state, held outside of time — waiting for the next time the eye would seek it out.

The booming shook my bones, reducing any semblance of hope I had left to nothing at all. My captors increased their hold on me, knowing what was to come. Their hot fingers dug deep into my flesh, the pain was terrible.

And then the eye found me.

Time slowed down. The hands holding me turned to stone. The black eye's gaze took hold of me with contemptuous ease. It bore into my skull, into my brain, into my memories, and found what it was looking for: every terrible moment of my life, every decision I had ever regretted, every mistake I had made, every memory of hurt I had caused or received ... It all rushed to the surface like a great well of poison. I relived it all, without pause, without respite. And I screamed.

It lasted weeks, perhaps months. I lost my sanity over and over again, only for the eye to bring me back to myself, to start the process again. It fed on my pain. It drew strength from this timeless suffering. If I could muster one coherent thought it was to wonder *what it was. Where did it come from?* But eventually that brief moment of lucidity was torn away and there was only endless suffering.

***

When I came to I was still held painfully aloft by my captors. The weeks that had passed — the near eternity of suffering that I had experienced — had in reality only taken a few seconds.

As the tower and its terrible eye rotated towards its next victim I spotted something strange: one of the pallid, hideous city dwellers that had originally paraded me about the streets, walked to the base of the coliseum walls. One of the many statuesque victims had dropped down, now fully fossilised, like a grotesque husk sucked dry. There wasn't anything left but bones of stone.

The creature picked up the fossilised remains, took them to the rotating tower, and threw them down a pit beneath the onyx base.

The entity, the structure with the eye, was like a millstone; grinding souls and bones to dust. It was a manifestation of evil beyond anything I could have imagined.

The leader of the city dwellers once again approached. He towered over me, seeming even taller than before, but perhaps this was because I could no longer stand unaided. He picked me up as if I was made of nothing substantial, a hollow man, easily discarded.

He whispered in my ears for some time, explaining the new reality of my life to me. We made a deal then, although that implies there was choice in the matter. The reality is that I would do anything, absolutely anything, to avoid the gaze of the thing on the onyx tower.

When my new role was understood I was dropped to the floor like an old rag. Yet I knew I had some value, and that was what was going to keep me free, unlike the poor souls who I would have to help collect to feed to that black eye.

And then it was over. I scrambled to my feet, sensing the walls starting to shift away, my own reality trying to spring back into focus.

Just before I returned to my dining room I spotted something still in the dream city which made my blood run cold one more time: Entering the coliseum through the red arch, of his own free accord unlike the pathetic manner in which I arrived, walked Jean-Pierre.

***

My purpose was now as clear as it was terrible: I had given them a foothold in our reality. Every time I turned my hourglass, their influence, their corrupting presence, manifested in our world for hours at a time. Their city would overlap with mine, invisible and undetected to all but those versed in its siren song.

 I can now see the denizens from the corner of my eye, out of time yet in our moment. Blurred but unmistakable, cackling with glee at their newfound freedom, no longer locked away in a distant pocket of time.

 Nobody else can see them. Nobody else knows that they are there, watching, scheming, and greedy.

 But that is not quite true is it? Jean-Pierre knows. It's his job to lure unsuspecting people to cross over and visit that central coliseum, to take the innocent and feed them to the creature at the heart of the city.

 I made the job so much easier for them. No longer do the victims have to travel to faraway deserts and dunes. The song is right here in the city; screams made melody, ancient doom made thunder. It just takes a small push for them to enter, as long as I keep turning the hourglass.

***

EPILOGUE

I saw Jean-Pierre one last time. I had taken to drinking heavily; jenever, beer, wine, I no longer cared. It was the only way that I could find sleep. My burden was such that I had developed a deep loathing within myself, a disgust of the enabler I had become. My own cowardice revolted me, but every time I thought I would do something to somehow make it stop I pictured myself hanging from the coliseum wall, unable to look away as the giant black eye settled its gaze on me. So I drank.

One evening, early still in my journey towards alcoholic oblivion, I noticed a weathered wraith of a man sat at a table in the back, hunched over a large glass of spirits. He stared at me, then looked at the ground. It was Jean-Pierre.

I joined him, uninvited, and was about to accost him for what he had done to me, when something in his demeanour arrested me. There were tears in his eyes, but only barely. I could see he had cried himself nearly dry. He grabbed both my hands and kissed them over and over. His lips were dry and cracked and somehow freezing cold.

"I had to do it ... I'm so sorry ... I tried to stop but, you've seen it. You know what it can do! But I'm sorry."

I did not answer. Instead I stared at his wrists. Deep gouges and scars crisscrossed his arms, and I realised that whatever I would say to him, or do to him, he was as much a prisoner as I was. I tried to soothe him, much to my own surprise. I think it was because I saw my own fate reflected in his eyes, and recognised the need for pity. Where else would we get it?

When I walked home I could see glimpses of the dream city from the corner of my eyes; flashes of merciless architecture, its deranged occupants a blur. It was intolerable.

I made a decision.

Back in my apartment I approached the hourglass. It towered over me with disdain. I knew I didn't have the strength to destroy it, nor would it let me. Even thinking about it made the screaming and booming swell, and the walls around me lose some of their solidity. Any act against the machine would see me drawn back into the dream city and dragged in front of the eye.

I pulled the crank once more, slowly starting the sands moving again. Did I hear a howl of victory?

Like a ghost I ascended the stairs to my loft. I sat in the multi-coloured light, basking in the sun. Somehow the dawn had arrived.

There was a knife there, an old present from Jean-Pierre.

Its edge was keen. It dug deep in my wrists. The pain was nothing to me.

Relief was a wave, washing away my guilt and pain, cleansing me of doubt. Until I saw what welled up from the wounds. I cut again, furiously, frantically, but the knife had dulled, my veins stopped flowing.

There was no blood, just red and ochre sand spilling out and collecting in two small heaps at my feet.

DEAR READER

My dear reader, finally we meet face to face. Or should I say, face to page? I must tell you that I cherish this moment. I feel that we're destined for each other, and now that our meeting is here it's like I've known you for many years. Like we're old friends, really.

Let me take a moment to confide in you:

From this moment onward, everything will be different for the both of us.

That's right, and I have to confess; it's hard to suppress my excitement at what is to come to pass. Truthfully, I cannot wait to tell you all about it.

You must forgive me my impatience; all will become clear shortly. It's just that I've been waiting for this moment — keening for it one might say — for the longest time. And now that our glorious rendezvous is finally taking place I almost cannot bear the sheer pleasure of observing your beautiful eyes as they pick out my words, and pluck them from the page like golden apples, ripe with promise.

Was that too much? I do apologise. My words are clumsy and crude, not quite up to the task of greeting you with the respect that you are due. The sad reality is that too much time has passed since I've spoken to anyone (anyone real that is), and I'm clearly out of practice.

I can see you have questions. This, my dear reader, or may I call you friend? This, is only natural. I will answer all your queries in due time, as I tell you my story. I promise you, it's quite a tale.

But before I get ahead of myself, I will answer one initial question, as it is vital that this is understood: please realise that I do not address anybody else but you, my dear reader. This is not metaphor, nor do I employ this word 'you' as if I were addressing a group of people. No, these words, these letters, these concepts are strictly for you, yourself, your person. And what a person you are! Your body so radiant, so comfortably corporeal, so full of life. I feel blessed that our fates are intertwined.

But there I go again, skipping to the end when I haven't explained the beginning. I really have forgotten all my manners, haven't I? Well, let me correct my errant behaviour at once, and tell you how I (we) came to this exact moment in our lives; this wonderful nexus of opportunity.

I will tell you my story.

***

I wasn't always like this. Oh no, there was a time when I had a beautiful body, like yours. It was male, and solid, and I think it was about 35 years old. I don't remember precisely, as certain events (that I will describe shortly) have put some strain on my memories. Truth be told, neither do I know how long ago all that happened. Lady Time has become a different character to me than the one I used to know. Does that make sense? I suspect not. But anyway, I remember enough to be able to tell you the key parts of the story. You can trust me, it's all true.

I used to work in a library in a great city. No, it doesn't matter which city, just that it had a grand library. You see, I was smitten with words even then. So much so that when I took my lunch breaks I took them in the library itself, so I could eat and read simultaneously, while surrounded by a plethora of wondrous books. Cheese sandwiches and thrillers, those were my favourites. I do wish I could taste a cheese sandwich again, and with your help I'm sure it will be so. (But I digress.)

One afternoon, no better or worse than any other afternoon, I took an especially delicious bite out of my granary and Stilton delight, and caught a glimpse of something quite disturbing out of the corner of my eye. For a moment (and it was surely no more than a flicker in time) I thought my right arm had become translucent. I could see right through the skin as if it were made of some organic form of glass, or perhaps a kind of ghost matter. But rather than seeing bones and sinew and muscle underneath, I spied another arm. This second arm was smaller, and sickly looking, with pasty skin and a mottled complexion.

This odd vision passed before I could examine it in any detail, and although it left me feeling somewhat puzzled I shrugged and pushed it out of my mind. I returned to my sandwich and thought no more of the matter.

When I finished work for the day the entire incident had fled my attention, as if it had never happened. Was it no more than a hallucination, perhaps caused by an overindulgence in cheese, on my part?

Ah, dear reader, would that it were so simple ...

***

The next day *the plot thickened*, as they say. (A clichéd expression for sure, but one that fits.)

As I stood in front of the mirror to attend to my morning grooming, another strange event occurred. I was shaving my throat (most carefully), and in the need to reach those awkward places, I had to peer askance at myself. When I lifted the razor to my jawline I once again glimpsed that same disturbing translucence that had befallen me the day before. I could see beneath the skin of my arm, and spotted the withered appendix I had seen the day before. Only this time I was able to maintain my view.

It was as if I had two bodies: an outer body — glorious and comfortable like yours, dear reader — and another hidden one, withered, diseased, wasting away. There was much evidence to support this: the mottled skin had gone even more grey. The fingers resembled claws of some vicious species of bird. And although this phantom arm had shrunk since I last saw it, I could also see more of its length, extending just beyond a bony elbow. I flexed my regular arm in wonder, yet two arms flexed in unison, one inside the other. Apparently they *both* belonged to me.

I dropped my razor in fright, and looked upon that accursed secondary limb directly, rather than through the mirror. This lessened the translucent effect to a great degree, but I could still just make out something underneath the skin.

In a panic (who could blame me), and not knowing what to do, I rang my physician and made an appointment to see him later that day, on the off chance that my strange experience could be attributed to a conventional medical cause. Perhaps something was amiss in my ocular system, causing these strange visual phenomena, or maybe something was causing pressure in my brain, leading to hallucinations. The latter thought scared me no end, dear reader, as I'm sure you can understand.

I spent half a day at work, trying to find comfort in books and words, but their soothing influence, normally so effective, eluded me. I was too scared to do much more than operate on instinct. I should note that curiously, yet somehow not surprisingly, nobody else saw anything out of the ordinary in my appearance. The phenomenon was reserved purely for my eyes only.

Morning and early afternoon passed in a daze, until it was time to leave for my appointment.

When I grabbed my coat and hat I caught another glimpse of that withering body underneath, but this time my left arm was affected by the translucency effect, revealing the other side of the phantom body I carried inside me.

I rushed down the streets, walking, then running, occasionally stumbling, for each time I looked at myself in the reflection of the shop windows beside me, two faces stared back at me. One I knew very well, as it was the same face I had seen each morning in the mirror for most of my life, but the other face was new, yet strangely familiar. It was small, like a child's, with haunting desperate eyes. It was the face of a creature condemned, fully aware of the disease eating away at its flesh, losing control of its very being.

I'm not ashamed to tell you my dear reader, (or may I call you friend?) that by the time I arrived at my physician's practice, I was overcome with sheer terror, barely able to contain myself while I took my repose in the waiting room. When I was finally called into the examination room I was jumping at every reflection, my nerves shredded, my composure all but lost.

The doctor was methodical and swift in his research, only slightly bemused by my strange symptoms. He asked precise and probing questions, peered into my eyes through that device doctors always use, the one with the red light. My ears were examined, my vitals were taken; heartbeat, blood pressure ... I shan't bore you with a full list of diagnostics employed to examine my affliction. In any event, it all amounted to a resounding declaration of health. Apparently there was nothing wrong with me on the surface of it. They would check the bloodworks, perhaps follow up with an x-ray, but I could see that none of that would lead anywhere. Whatever was happening to me was not to be explained in medical terms.

***

I shall now, with your permission I hope, skip through the next few days to aid the telling of this story. Suffice to say that my situation got gradually worse, insofar that my entire body, every inch of my skin, became a window through which I could observe that damned other body.

Over the following weeks I tried to do my own medical research, hoping to shine a light on this mystery. But no matter how much I read, nothing seemed to fit. I even studied a number of occult tomes, the names of which are best left unsaid. Again, there were no clues about my unfolding fate, other than those I observed myself.

The body underneath my skin was deteriorating. Its skin no longer just a mottled grey, but riddled with black sores. Arms, legs, and torso took on a wasted appearance, starving away, deprived somehow of the sustenance needed to maintain itself.

But worst of all was that face ... It resembled me, like a close relative, but as the days ran away from me it took on a most frightening, even demonic appearance: its skin stretched taut, causing the teeth to stand out in a skeletal grin. Eyes sunk into deep sockets, almost (but not quite) hiding a maniacal intelligence. It was entirely bald, nor could I discern facial hair of any kind, lending the face a surreal, ageless quality. I was convinced that I looked into the eyes of pure evil, waiting for something, calmly but with increasing appetite.

It is hard to describe the sheer dread and despair I felt, unable to understand what was happening to me. Many times did I consider taking my own life, such was my anguish. I think nobody could have thought ill of me for doing so, but somehow I clung on, at least until the Other started asserting itself, at which point it was too late, and I was beyond help.

***

The takeover started small, and initially went unnoticed.

I increasingly found myself lost in daydreams, suffering distractions more readily than I used to, but then; what else was to be expected considering my circumstances? I started sleepwalking, occasionally snapping out of strange dreams and finding myself out in the night in unexpected places: standing next to my bookcase, or having walked to work, or holding a dictionary. You may have detected a connecting element to these disparate events?

The daydreams became performative, by which I mean that I caught myself doing things without any conscious thought behind it, as if somebody else was controlling my actions at the times when I was absentminded. Again, these moments would always revolve around the written word: I'd find myself reading a novel I had not consciously chosen, or buying an unknown textbook in a book store.

While all this was going on, the evil presence residing in the Other's body seemed to lose substance. Perhaps it was dying, as its body continued to wither and waste away apace.

Then, one day, I crossed a barrier of sorts, with unimaginably horrific consequences. It happened after yet another performative daydream, this time at my place of work. Without realising it I had wondered off to a part of the library containing esoteric texts filled with mystic musings and tales of horror and woe. All very Gothic dear reader, and some of it more than a little gauche.

On previous occasions I would snap out of it, go back to whatever I was doing before, and that would be that. But not this time. When I willed myself to return to my work nothing happened. Far from it! I continued to browse and skim the tomes on offer, ignoring the decision I thought I had made. It was as if my brain had been disconnected from the rest of me.

Initially I thought my body had become autonomous, perhaps working on instinct, but eventually the abhorrent truth became clear to me: the Other, the decrepit and evil passenger inside me, had swapped its consciousness with mine, so that I no longer had any control over my original body.

I knew this to be true, as an animal instinctively knows when it's trapped or dying. Yet, for many painful hours did I hold out some hope that this was merely temporary, or that I was now hallucinating on a whole different plane of madness. These hopes were cruelly dashed later that day, after my body had left work and gone home to my apartment.

Who - or *what*ever was driving my body - used my toilet facilities (as embarrassing an experience as I have ever had to suffer) and dutifully washed his/my hands afterwards. At that point our gazes met in the mirror, as they did before, but now our situation was reversed. My outer body, my real body, still featured its translucent skin, through which I could see myself, floating inside a red void. I knew it was me because I could see the horror of recognition express itself on the face of the withered corpus inside, while the face of my real body had taken on a demonic quality, and wore a cruel, knowing grin.

***

I had become a prisoner, trapped in the Other's body, without agency or recourse, forced to watch this evil entity take over my life like some grotesque cuckoo. It seemed perfectly at ease with my work requirements, conversed convincingly with my friends, even with members of my family. Nobody was the wiser. The Other had become the *Impostor*.

But whenever we were alone it would grin that knowing grin, and I felt afraid, for my new body was still wasting away, and I had no idea what would become of me.

The degenerative process seemed to be speeding up in a matter of days, and soon my withered, helpless form was *shrinking*. It was another terrifying process (as if I had not experienced enough fear) because as I got physically smaller, the world around me underwent a metamorphosis ... My environment became one suited for giants only; objects and spaces took on huge, even gargantuan dimensions. I knew this was just a relative change, it merely seemed that way due to my own reduced stature, akin to *trompe l'oeil*, but it was no less disturbing for it. Imagine my dear friend what that must feel like!

The Impostor eventually stopped looking at me for I had diminished to a point that was beneath its notice. Oh how I missed its evil grin at that moment. Mocking and cruel it had been, but at least it recognised me for being of some consequence.

Curiously, this thief, this evil thing, maintained its interest in books and words. It spent most of its time alone reading. This fact did not stand out as noteworthy to me at first, especially as I had deeper worries to contend with; *How small would I become? Would I simply cease to exist eventually?* Well my dearest reader, my dear friend; the answer would come soon enough, and in a manner that will matter a great deal to you on a very personal level.

I can't wait to share. Soon you will know all.

***

After enduring weeks of helpless co-existence with the Impostor, I almost made peace with my lot, which ironically led to a momentous revelation ... It happened for the most mundane of reasons; not being able to influence events even slightly, I was slowly becoming bored. This may surprise you dear reader, but when one is completely helpless, when one's situation appears unlikely to change, then one's mind starts to crave nourishment. It needs something to engage with or it wilts like a forgotten flower. I found such relief by partaking in the Impostor's reading habit.

The real world had become insubstantial to me, immersed as I was under the skin of my old body. It was like perpetually living under water, muffled and separated from the world above. I almost entered a fugue-like state, if it weren't for frequent exposure to the written word. I don't understand how, but I maintained the ability to read along with whatever my captor was reading. Book covers stood out like a homing beacon, the words inside the covers rich and textural. There was a connection there that I hadn't noticed before. A whole world existed between the letters, underneath the pages, between the paragraphs — and it called out to me. I gladly answered that summons.

No my friend, I do not speak in metaphors ... I could literally inhabit this literary environment. My essence, my soul if you will, entered each book, each text, each treatise, and traversed its depths. Some text were vertiginous, with sentences and clauses like skyscrapers — prose looming like mountains. Others were as deep and vast as the ocean, interspersed with little islands of wit and erudition. The letters themselves were slabs of obsidian, forming dark cities of ink, endless forests of typography.

I became quite adept at travelling these places. Things work differently in that world. A person can manipulate the rules by changing a word here, a comma there. There were many secrets in between the pages I travelled. Many truths, untruths, forbidden knowledge and unspeakable lore. The real world, your meat-world my dear friend, lost its interest to me. I craved new texts, new worlds to explore. I cursed the Impostor whenever it stopped reading, forcing me back inside the wasted shell of a body it made me inhabit. These abrupt separations from word-spaces left me screaming with frustration, like a broken machine. I just wanted to return to the books — the only place that now felt real to me, where I could be of consequence again. I cried fevered tears of relief each time the Impostor picked up a book again, so I could explore once more.

My travels taught me much. Things for which I lack adequate vocabulary, so I can't describe them to you. But I can tell you that I steadily grew in strength and cunning, until one day I discovered a secret that allowed me to break free.

***

So, friend, we are nearing the conclusion of this story. Not quite what you expected is it? Stay with me, I have more surprises in store for you.

This realm that I had entered, this dimension of ink and stories, was much larger than it initially appeared. At first I imagined each book to be a self-contained place. I could roam their ebon structures and dark pathways within the confines of the text, but no further. But I learned that this was wrong. Painfully wrong as it turned out. Soon, you will know this too sir.

One day I reached the end of a book before the Impostor did, where I discovered a thin membrane — not quite opaque — hinting at something beyond. I pushed through, revealing a secret: The book-spaces I had so frequently and innocently entered, connected to a much larger world, or dimension, or whatever word one would use to describe that gloomy and ancient place.

I wish I could show it to you my 'friend' ... A giant, dark star straddles an ashen sky, and illuminates absolutely nothing. No warmth rides its lightless rays. It is completely stationary. Everything one sees is made of shadows and blackness. A layer of grey dust smothers all. It comes from a frequent rain of ash, gushing out of sick clouds. There are few animals or plants — a grub here, a thorny creeper there — barely surviving in the fetid soil.

One can see farther than should be possible, surveying the entire dimension in a single glance, despite its frightening size. Peer long and deep enough and one's sanity starts to crumble. But this mode of sight was valuable to me, as it revealed that other books and texts and scripture and everything that was ever written down, connected to this lonely, awful place. I could enter those other texts with ease, and just like that I was free from the Impostor. How about that sir? Didn't think I could escape did you? Well, I did, and here I am, talking to you.

Distance means little to me now. I can flit from book to text to manual to psalm instantly, for the dimension of dark words connects all. I travelled like this for a long time, learning many things. But what was I to do now? I was finally free, this is true, but at what cost?

Yes, I called it a lonely place, but I was not alone.

***

Scared you, didn't I? Good. I want you to be scared my 'friend', it adds spice to our story.

I'm nearly finished, and that means so are you. Let's wrap this drama up shall we? I'm tired of speaking to you. But I will persist till the end.

The dimension of dark words is ancient. I suspect it came into existence the first time primitive people wrote a message with hatred in their heart, many many thousands of years ago. Perhaps it was a curse, or an expression of blasphemy. It doesn't matter, as it was now my world.

And while I was free from the Impostor, I was also trapped inside this cursed place, for I had no body in your world to return to. My initial elation at being free turned to despair. I slogged through avenues of doomed word clusters and crumbling wordplay for eternities. I climbed mountains of grey soil and ink-dust. My despair turned to anger. White hot and bitter.

I raged; what had I ever done to deserve this? I just wanted to love my books, eat my cheese sandwiches. Look at me now 'friend'! All the colour, and life and substance has been drained from me.

They found me you see? The others who had been trapped here before me. Some have been here for a thousand years, maybe longer. My anger was a beacon for them. Something new and noteworthy in a place bereft of any texture and interest. Some taught me new things, we shared our experience and knowledge. Others are so empty and soulless that they can't help but attack anything new. They try to suck me dry, take what little life force I have left, for themselves.

This place is hell. There is no other word for it.

And I am so angry. And so hungry. I need a body. I need a soul. I need light. I need to touch.

The final secret, 'FRIEND', is that I have been watching you. This place, where we can see the entire realm from any vantage point, also allows us to catch glimpses of people on the other side, peering in, blind, unknowing. People like you, sir. Not often — for time works differently here — and not very clear most of the time. But once in a while a reader shows up with whom one of us has a *connection*. And with careful work and patience this connection can be cultivated, strengthened, until it becomes a tether, the kind that binds.

I have attached myself to you with just such a tether. It's quite unbreakable, I can assure you. It will grow stronger each time you read something; a book, a magazine, a recipe, a bloody shopping list will do. IT DOESN'T MATTER! I have you now!

Slowly I will pull myself towards you. Towards your warm, comfortable body. My unending rage gives me the strength and endurance to accomplish this. After all these years I will finally escape! It is inevitable.

You will take my place, and I will take yours.

I will enter you. You will be able to see me through your skin. And you will recognise me by the hatred in my smile.

THE BALLROOM UNDER THE LAKE

I am just like you, yet I am not.

Yes, it's true that when I smash my forehead against a wall, a bruise dutifully appears the next day, colourful and brash. Gently push a sowing needle through a pinched arc of skin on my forearm, and a drop of blood proudly wells in reward. And when I bite down fiercely on the meaty part of my hand, ghostly tooth prints appear, soon filled with red as displaced blood returns to its home.

I know these things to be true; I have tested their veracity on countless occasions, just as I have tested other methods of harm, each offering their own small award. In this, I am no different from you, but — despite this superficial similarity — I am denied each and every time what I truly crave; the elusive and humanising charm of *pain*.

CIPA disease means that my nerve endings have not developed properly, like yours have. I can feel no pain, no matter how bad the hurt or severe the injury. I wager that your thoughts right now reflect a certain amount of envy, or at least curiosity, do they not?

What would it be like if I felt no pain? It doesn't sound that bad ... A life without physical agony ... what's the downside?

Those are natural thoughts. Most people feel this way when they find out about my affliction, even if only for a fleeting moment. But — as is the case with many things in life — people don't understand the value of a thing until it is lost.

***

Reginald. Even his name entertains.

If I could create a perfect counter image to myself — a complete opposite manifestation, possessing all the good traits I lack, yet unencumbered with my most egregious flaws — I would construct a being such as Reginald. He is everything I wish to be and has achieved everything I aspire to myself.

This doesn't mean I see no value at all in myself; despite my bouts of low self-esteem and existential angst, I feel that we complement each other in ways that create a partnership which outshines its constituting parts. My stubbornness and perseverance counter Reginald's flighty nature, while his good looks and penetrating charm open doors normally closed to me.

None of this would matter if we hadn't aligned as much as we did through our shared professional and personal interests:

I've always been deeply attracted to (and at times delighted by) the phenomenon of historic, architectural 'follies'; those strange and bizarre constructs created by eccentrics through the ages, motivated by strong passions fuelled by occult delusions or deeply romantic notions. I have dedicated my life to researching and writing about these oddities, precisely because of my own inability to make sense of the human condition. I suppose it gives me comfort that there have been many souls before me as adrift as mine, or at least moored on the edges of acceptable thought and behaviour.

Reginald has a passion similar to mine, but more akin to the modern concept of 'urban spelunking'; the practice of discovering (and exploring) abandoned and lost places. He's made a career of tracking down and photographing the most extraordinary forgotten buildings and lost structures, infused with secret histories, hinting at liminal spaces and possessing of ephemeral qualities.

We work well together. Reginald effortlessly commands a network of oddballs, freaks, rich outcasts and outsiders who feed him exciting new clues and leads on a near-daily basis, while I'm as determined a researcher of old texts and records and other historic data as one is likely to find. Once I pick up a scent I will not rest until I have hunted it down to its source and subdued it into revealing its secrets.

Many of Reginald's finds lead not just to obscured architectural marvels but also to completely unknown, fascinating follies, while my dogged efforts have uncovered the existence of more noteworthy, orphaned architectural marvels than Reginald would ever find on his own, despite his many talents.

Sometimes our interests and research overlap so perfectly that we need but a nod and a grunt to embark on a joined expedition. Those are moments when both our lives make sense.

***

Reginald sings loudly. I mutter for him to be quiet. Not with real anger or irritation — in fact I feel a great deal of affection for his ability to fill the damp, sooted corridor with a modicum of cheer. Nonetheless, it's unwise to create a spectacle when illegally entering an abandoned building. Uncowed and with a mocking spring in his step Reginald beckons me to follow him.

Like many Victorian buildings, the textile factory is both a study in grandeur and grotesquerie. It's hard not to notice the requisite, vertiginously tall ceilings, immaculate woodwork detailing, ornate window designs, and a real flair for wrought iron machinery. Yet throughout the impressive (and it must be said oppressive) structural detail runs a subtle strain of dread and cruelty.

Sepia toned photos of blank faced children adorn the walls, depicting the little ones next to sharp-edged cotton processing machines. My research identifies these souls as 'scavengers'; children tasked with cleaning the machines as they ran, frequently losing fingers or worse in the process. We pass a collection of crude, linen masks lying in a heap; cheap efforts at keeping the all-but-indentured workers from literally choking to death on the dust and heat during their twelve hours shifts. And finally, we encounter an abysmal chapel with a terrible past; the reason for my personal interest in this expedition.

Back in those days the church was frequently involved in industry, providing special services to the 'men of distinction' who ran such places. There was always demand for the church's special workforce, rented out for a few coppers a day to the factories and the workhouses. The workers were the children of the poor — abandoned by despairing parents, unwilling to see their offspring succumb to the same demons in life as they did. They were also the 'fallen mothers' who had the misfortune of being young and suffering disapproved pregnancy — the fathers having disappeared for the typical reasons these men always run away. Children and young women forced into endless, brutal labour, to advance the glory of the church.

"This is just right for you, Emrys," says Reginald.

"I think so too," I reply, studying the black, onyx obelisk at the centre of the chapel. "It's quite an extraordinary find."

"I thought you'd like it. Grim and weird, just like you."

"This obelisk hasn't been seen in a hundred years," I say, ignoring Reginald's customary insults. "It was a stipulation of the factory owner that the chapel be constructed around it, and that it would be used as a shaming device for sinful souls."

"What does that even mean? And please, for once, talk like a person, not an old musty book."

"They punished people here. Made them lean over, put their hands on the obelisk, and cane them."

"Really?"

"Or sometimes force them to stand like that for hours on end."

"Bugger them?" asks Reginald as he bends forward and demonstratively assumes the described pose himself. His lusty tone and provocative stance so inappropriate that I have to laugh. It's typical of him, and indicative of his voracious sexual appetite and insatiable urges. Reginald pursues vice with a tenacity only matched by the breadth of his taste.

Female or male, younger or older than him, racial background, sexual eccentricities ... none of these things matter to him. He will do anything with anybody, or *to* anybody, as long as he finds them interesting on some level, or at least entertaining.

I say; "Let's set up your camera gear," attempting to get his mind back on the job. 'I'll need a photo of this for our article.' But Reginald's attention is diverted. His elegant, dark fingers, almost invisible against the onyx obelisk, push off and he straightens.

"Emrys? What's th—" Abruptly Reginald falls silent and he moves to an adjacent room, door left ajar. I glimpse moonlit shapes, unrecognisable yet somehow familiar in a sickening way; like remembering an old nightmare, dormant for years but reaching up from that deep, bottomless well in our mind where such things hide, to resume terrorising your sleep.

***

Limbs, torsos, legs, hands silently clawing at the air, decrepit and dirty nails flashing in the meagre light. A giant heap, scores and scores of shapes, reaching as high as the top of the windows. A mound of madness, untouched for years.

Reginald speaks — I can see his mouth move — but I can't listen. A booming, deafening pulse rages in my head, batters down a door in me, releasing a thing of dread. A memory that is not a memory, a fear that is not a fear. A raw, haunting thing that slowly drags itself towards my conscious awareness.

Reginald walks towards the mound, his dark shape outlined by a silver rim of pure moonlight. I raise my hand, as if to stop him, but he's far beyond my reach. My jaw clicks harshly as I open my mouth to shout a warning — a consequence of a badly healed fracture I once ignored for too long. I never felt the pain that would have told me it needed attention.

But before I can make a sound, Reginald kicks the mound with surprising force. A hand and lower arm detach and skitter across the dark, shale stone floor, coming to a stop, mere inches from my right foot.

"Bloody mannequins," says Reginald. "Hundreds of them."

"From the factory ..." I stammered.

"Yes, *from the factory*," the reply comes in a sing-song imitation of my shaking voice. Reginald kicks another limb from the mound, which partially collapses, making a terrible racket, echoing down the corridor behind us.

"Stop ... please ..." I barely recognise my own voice.

My words achieve the opposite to their intention; evoking a blind rage in Reginald instead. He kicks the grim mound again and again, grunting with the effort of it, until dozens of limbs and torsos and broken heads litter the floor around us. Shaking uncontrollably, Reginald picks up a forearm, an elegantly manicured hand still attached, mocking his brutish rage. He repeatedly smashes it against the floor, like a primitive ancestor of humanity discovering the deliciously destructive power of using a bone as a weapon. Splinters and debris explode from the repeated impact; I feel several shards hit my face but of course feel no pain.

"Stop!" I shout this time. "Control yourself!"

Reginald freezes, throws me a piercing, contemptuous sneer. "You should try feeling emotions one day. It might help you hang on to a woman for once."

His words sting. Judith only left me a few weeks ago.

There is a cruel side to Reginald, an acid that occasionally burns through the shiny veneer glossing the easy-going character he shows everyone, all the more painful because nobody expects it from him. To know Reginald is to first love him, then suffer heartbreak. This is why he has no real friends other than me. Nobody can stand to be in his shade when he previously lit them up like the sun.

It doesn't bother me, because I know where it comes from; I know that beyond the charm, the good looks, the humour, the endless capacity for partying and socialising and sex and all of that, Reginald is as empty inside as I am. And I know that he needs to fill that void, like I do. I know that he is as dumbfounded by human behaviour as I am. This is why I'm not jealous of my friend, despite his qualities, and never will be. Who would be jealous of that?

***

It takes an hour to photograph all we need. Reginald is a wizard with a camera, but shooting at night means setting up lights and carefully planning shots. By the time we're done, both of us are exhausted but content, our demons retreated for now.

We retrace our steps through the factory, back to the old, forgotten supply hatch that provided us with an entry. The sky is turning purple, like a new bruise, threatens us with dawn.

"No hard feelings? About earlier?" Remorse and shyness make a mockery of

Reginald's carefully constructed persona. I feel oddly proud he dares to show me his true face.

"I thought you wanted me to try feeling emotions?"

"You *are* an odd duck Emrys."

"What does that make you?"

"As fabulous as ever."

I laugh, despite myself, then fall silent. *Did I hear something?* I raise my index finger to my lips, then cup a hand to my ear and wait.

The wind murmurs and whispers beyond the hatch. A faraway dog barks faintly. The booming pulse in my head quietly echoes from deep within.

"We should be careful ..."

Reginald pulls an exasperated face but holds his tongue. We slowly open the hatch into the night. It is July, the air is hot and humid, but I don't sweat because I can't. CIPA disease comes with anhydrosis, as it does with other unexpected side effects.

The hatch leads to a narrow, damp alley, overrun with weeds sprouting between the pieces of broken glass and vintage bricks that litter the ground. Our shoes crunch loudly as we walk. The alley gives way to a mostly barren piece of industrial land, gated and padlocked, except for a concealed hole in a fence, a hundred yards ahead. We're alone but for the corpse of an old rusted truck, lying on its side near the exit like an old animal that collapsed and died a long time ago. A small tree sprouts straight from the cab at the front. A single bird excitedly chitters and chatters, trying to tell us about the arrival of a new day, now almost upon us.

"Come on," I whisper, and set off.

Reginald follows by my side, for once failing to offer a barbed comment.

We make it halfway across the grounds when two figures step from behind the truck. Their widening grins appear as if painted on, dripping with malice and anticipation. I know I will be a disappointment to them.

"Oh dear," says Reginald, not quite keeping the fear from his voice.

The guards place themselves between our position and the hole in the fence, jog toward us. It seems they are eager to punish.

"Stay behind me," I hiss at Reginald, who obeys without comment.

The first guard is unnaturally tall and muscular, but thin, as if elongated artificially. The second guard is heavy set, but endowed with a set of shoulders as impressive as his mighty gut. Both look formidable in their own way.

The tall guard reaches us first, swings at me. I deliberately let him punch my face. He shrieks in pain, his hand likely broken. While he's distracted, I kick his kneecap, doing some damage from the crunching sound of it, enough to give him pause. The second guard now arrives, panting and sweating, but careful with his approach after seeing what happened to his friend. I judge him to be the more dangerous one as he cuts off our path to the exit.

Reginald instinctively flanks him, forcing the guard to choose who to engage with first. He chooses me, spreading his arm in a ridiculous fighting stance, like some kind of ancient wrestler. He slowly advances, while Reginald drifts off further and further to the right of me.

To my dismay I realise that guard one has regained his mobility, although his right hand flops uselessly by his side. Unfortunately, he appears to be ambidextrous, deftly handling a serrated knife with his other hand. I glance at Reginald, feeling like we're running out of time.

"The tall one ... together ..." Reginald nods, then feints a move to his right, left, right again, then runs past the tall guard's mangled right hand, staying out of reach of the knife in his left. It's a perfectly executed move, expertly crowned by a vicious punch to the guard's broken hand. He howls, swings his knife wildly, but Reginald is already far out of reach.

Guard number two is now right in front of me. A sweating, hulking thing; blubber and muscle competing to define the man's shape. He grabs me with both hands, thinking his freakish size and strength will give him the upper hand. I allow him to entertain that thought as he draws me into a crushing bear hug. He laughs wordlessly, brainlessly, nearly overwhelming me with a stench of garlic, beer, and sweat.

"I've got this little shit!" he shouts to his partner, who is still clutching his broken hand. Of Reginald there is no trace.

"I've got you now, you little sh—" Guard two doesn't finish his redundant comment, as I first pull backward — dragging him with me until he is forced to push back — then quickly step forward and smash my forehead into his bulbous nose with as much force and speed as I can muster, destroying it completely. Even before he can raise his hands to touch his ruined nose I repeat my move, now connecting with his forehead. He sways, a stupid expression in his face, hands wavering between touching his pulped nose or his ripped upper lip. A final head-butt breaks his cheekbone. He voids his bowels, and crumples.

Reginald — the coward who is also my only friend — has almost reached the fence. He glances backwards one time only, then climbs through the hole, leaving me alone with the guards.

The image of the tall guard's mangled hand does something to me. I flash back to the broken mannequins in the textile factory. The nameless thing of dread which stalks my subconscious mind, threatening to break through to awareness. The pulsing, booming noise in my head. My jaw clicks sharply as I open my mouth wide with laughter.

***

I'm in my loft apartment. I wash my face in the sink with hot water, using a thermometer to make sure I don't scold myself. Steam settles on the old-fashioned mirror, revealing just how dirty it is. I rinse several times, struggling to wash off the blood caking my face, my hair. There is a lot of it. None of it is mine.

The skin of my hands is scratched and beaten, curiously reminding me of shark skin. The tall guard won't be able to speak for some time, but I think they can save his sight.

I push my sodden fringe away from my forehead. Red-streaked water drips along the cracks in the off-white, ceramic bowl. I wipe my forehead. Something scratches my hand: a tooth, firmly embedded. It takes a surprising amount of effort to dislodge it. I think I should feel guilt, but all I can muster is a deep sense of melancholy and tiredness.

This is why Judith left me. This is why Reginald's barb felt so cruel, because he was right. I don't feel enough. CIPA disease is like that; without pain there is a muffled quality to life. Without sweat my own body feels alien to me. Even my sense of taste and smell are affected, leaving me unable to summon the kind of enthusiasm for food that some people are capable of.

Judith told me that living with me was like 'living with a bad photocopy of a person'. All the elements are there, all the features, but faded and two-dimensional. She called it 'Dissociative Personality Disorder'. At the time I thought she was being overly dramatic, that she couldn't possibly experience life so differently, so *vividly*, compared to me. But then another thought hit me. How would I know? *How could I imagine what I couldn't experience?*

What if this was like asking a blind person to understand colour? Or a deaf person to understand music? *What is it really like to be a normal person?*

It's a question I have no answer for, which in its way is its own answer.

***

For two days I exist in a fugue state, contained in my loft, silent and alone. My thoughts form a slow moving, giant whirlpool, rotating around a past I don't dare examine in detail. Images of rotting mannequins — their wooden claws reaching for me — surface briefly, sink back into oblivion, temporarily replaced by flashes of sharp-edged machinery, masked children, young women gripping a black obelisk ... It is hard to judge time, it does what it wills with me.

When Reginald finally drops by, he brings chocolates and brusquely shoves them at me. As always, his attempts at even mild apology are pitiful. Reginald wears contrition like an uncomfortable, dirty coat, and soon discards it completely. It's just not his style.

"Good news first, or bad news?"

"Good news please," I reply. It's what I always say. Reginald knows this, and takes advantage of our little rituals to put me at ease.

"Good news it is. Tada!" He hands me a thick envelope. Inside I find about two dozen photos of the textile factory and the obelisk folly. They are stunning.

"I'll start writing a piece to go with them," I say, feeling some genuine excitement, until Reginald gives me an odd look. "How bad is the bad news?" I ask.

"Quite bad, but not insurmountable."

"What?"

"We can't publish these for now. Maybe never."

"Why?"

"You are quite a character Emrys. You keep surprising me."

"Just ... why?"

"Those guards! How did you manage to mess them up so much? One is in a coma — the one that looked like a bull — the other one is ... *unrecognisable* ... but will probably live."

"Well, he had a knife, and I had no backup." I spit the last word at Reginald, but the implied accusation bounces off his ego shield without leaving a mark.

"Had to save the camera and negatives, or we would've done it all for nothing. Besides, I knew you'd handle those boys. Didn't think you'd go quite that far though."

I look at the prints. "These are terrific, I must say ..." I hold them up against the hazy, yellow light falling through the loft's dusty skylight. "I'll write the article. The guards will recover and I want to write it when everything is still fresh in my mind. We can sell the piece in twelve months when nobody will care about how we got these."

"You're a cold bastard," laughs Reginald.

"And what does that make you?"

"Fabulous as ever."

Our rituals comfort me. I smile. Reginald, satisfied that I don't bear a grudge for his running off, taps his wrist.

"I must fly dear chap. Try not to stew in here too long."

"New conquest?"

"A wavering priest, no less. The guilt adds a delicious note of spice to the sex."

"Whose guilt? His or yours?"

"I'll tell you when I figure that out myself. In the meantime, try and loosen up a bit. I mean it."

"I'll do some sketching. That always helps. Maybe some research for our next project?" I notice a glint in Reginald's eyes. More so than usual.

"What?"

"I wasn't going to say ... in case it doesn't pan out ..."

"What?!" I laugh. "Spit it out, you can't keep anything to yourself anyway."

Reginald theatrically holds his chin, as if seriously contemplating sharing whatever he's hiding from me. "Perhaps I should ... Hmm ... Not sure ..." He's being a tease, a role he enjoys too much.

"Get on with it!" I roar, mock-threatening him with a raised fist.

A tiny flicker of unease touches his face, soon replaced with Reginald's patented rakish expression which he reserves for moments where he has to be at his most charming.

"I'll tell you this: I may have a lead to something truly, gloriously special. I won't say what just yet — don't want to get your hopes up — but if it comes through — still an *if*, mind you — then you'll thank me, and forgive me for everything I have ever done to you."

With that he rushes out the door, ignoring my pleas for more information, leaving behind a strangely beguiling scent of linseed oil and sandalwood.

***

I produce two articles.

The first one is just what's expected of me; a well-researched essay on the Victorian textile factory's history, anecdotes of its time interspersed with witty commentary through a more modern, *enlightened* lens. Paired with Reginald's photos the piece proudly showcases a professional sheen, almost effortless in evoking the required sense of awe and drama, while politely touching upon titillating elements of the grotesque and esoteric. The Fortean Times would likely buy this piece as it fits their high standards perfectly. I feel a vague, uneasy mix of pride and shame for having written it.

The second article is something else entirely. I sit down, and start sketching without plan or thought. Mannequins ... broken hands ... hollow eyes ... I let the flow of images take me back to the factory, the chapel, the guards.

Words and drawings fall out of me, not so much written as birthed in a painful, drawn-out, fever dream. I lose sense of time, of my loft space, of my body, gripped in an escalation of the whirlpool of imagery that had gripped me before. But now, it feels more like a tornado; an immense, deafening force spinning me round while eagerly sucking a stream of emotions and ideas and epiphanies and fears and joys and sweat and pain from my helpless body.

    I try to fight it at first, but soon give in to the experience and watch myself being drained. I am an outsider to my own life, looking in without comprehension.

***

I hang motionless in a damp, endless void. I am aware and I am not. Time passes and it does not. Sensory input is almost completely lacking, not just an absence of pain, of warmth and cold, but of any discernible sensation, until — almost shocking in its specificity — a familiar scent snakes itself into my awareness. With it comes light, sound, and motion. A hand shakes my shoulder, a voice speaks my name. Sandalwood and linseed oil ride Reginald's breath as he attempts to wake me.

    I remain mute for some time as he chatters at me, like a pet bird, oblivious to my inability to speak.

"Been a bit naughty with the old Valium have you, Emrys? Not heard from you for weeks! I didn't think you had the stomach for such *indulgences*. Take it from me, there's better stuff out there, more fun and less soporific."

Reginald picks up some of my sketches, frowns at the outlandish, furious drawings and symbols as he prattles on. "Hah, *soporific* … starting to sound just like you. That won't do at all!" Slowly the stream of words ceases, a look of alarm appears on Reginald's face.

"That's not for the article," I say, my voice croaky from lack of use.

Reginald nearly drops the sketch in surprise.

"You're awake! Good!" He puts the sketch down, quickly forgotten.

"I was sleeping … I dreamed of—"

"Yes yes, that's all very interesting, but all that can wait."

"Wait? For what?"

"For our expedition. I was right; I found us something incredible. We're going today."

"Today? How—"

Reginald grabs my shoulders, shakes. "What is, the matter with you Emrys? And these ghastly drawings?"

"I had the strangest—"

"No, never mind. You're clearly in a funk and need to get rescued from your stuffy loft by no one other than me. Don't worry, I have already packed all we need."

***

Reginald drives his flashy, classic car — some kind of 1960s' sporty convertible — without real skill in terms of handling, but with a flair for showing off. The July afternoon sun is bright and hot, and the open roof gives me some welcome relief. Without the ability to sweat, cars can be dangerous to me.

Reginald looks happy as we leave the comforting embrace of the city, and enter a world of grand estates with long entrance drives and sprawling grounds, connected by winding country lanes in between. The idyll of our surroundings is only marred by the occasional piece of roadkill that one inevitably encounters in such places.

"You're in for a treat my friend," beams Reginald. "Guests of Poseidon, no less. Or was it Neptune?"

"You enjoy confusing me, don't you?"

"A bit of drama, a bit of excitement ... It's what keeps a man truly alive. You're lucky to have me, and remind you of these things."

"I'm excited! I'm alive! Now please tell me where we're going!"

For this I receive a disapproving look, but Reginald is far too eager and proud of his special find to keep me in the dark for long.

"Fine, fine, it's a folly, but not like any you've ever seen. I got a tipoff from this deliciously scandalous socialite, a duchess no less, who owns a neighbouring property or something like that. You know; 'old money, new debt' type? She's proven herself quite resourceful. The things this woman can do with a simple candle ..."

"Wait, what happened to the priest?"

"I got bored with the guilt trips. It's always the same with these catholic types. Who has time for that? Anyway ... she knows about this place because these old, rich families bear old and rich grudges, and they had a long-running one with their neighbours from way back in the day."

"What was it? A topiary dispute? A fox hunt incident?" I struggle to keep the disdain from my voice.

Another searing glance from Reginald. "Try and not be too jealous of your betters, old chap." It takes an exaggerated wink for me to realise he's having me on, before he continues; "It was the folly. That's what makes it so delicious. Apparently, their neighbour, an eccentric widow, married some upstart entrepreneur who had come into lots and lots of money. This was in the 1890s or so. They pooled their resources and re-landscaped the grounds, expanded the estate, throwing millions and millions at it. Caused a lot of disturbance and nuisance of course, and many of the additions were rather vulgar apparently, but that wasn't the worst of it."

"Here comes the topiary incident ..."

"Will you stop it?"

I raise my hands in surrender; "Tell me then. So far this makes no sense whatsoever."

"I'll do something better ... I'll *show* you."

The car slows down, Reginald turns into a narrow nondescript drive, flanked by thick, stumpy trees. Potholes, bumps, fallen tree logs, indicate this is not a popular path. I politely wait until we arrive at a wooden gate. Reginald gets out, opens the gate with some effort. "Nearly there now," he grunts.

We drive slowly into the setting sun, the tree-flanked road completely shielding our destination as well as our origin. I feel claustrophobic, suppress a spiking sense of irritation.

We turn a final corner to arrive at an old, derelict carriage house, where Reginald parks his ludicrously out of place, show-off car beneath the rotting, wooden beams. He steps out, impatiently tells me to follow him.

"This way," he points at a dried-up, old mud path that branches away from the drive which continues elsewhere. Presumably to the estate.

"Amazing ..." mutters Reginald, setting forth down the path. "Just where the lovely duchess told me it would be."

***

The mud has dried in a pattern of hexagonal cracks, like those one would expect in an African savanna during the dry season. My shoes soon carry a coat of brown dust, as we follow the path up a long, gradual slope. I feel like a pilgrim in a strange land.

I can tell that Reginald is in an excited mood — his stride eager and impatient — but I can't help but feel somewhat ambivalent about his claims. What folly can possibly exist out here to warrant this kind of anticipation? But then again, there's no denying the glint in Reginald's eyes or the flush in his cheek.

We reach the edge of the slope where our view is finally no longer constrained. The sun behind us throws our lengthening shadows towards the silver, sparkling mirror of a lake.

"Good, we're here," says Reginald.

"I don't understand," I say, looking around me. "Where is your glorious folly?"

"Look carefully ... see there, the middle of the lake ..."

Bathed in dancing, glittering reflections, a lone figure rises dramatically from the water, appearing to stand on its surface as if by magic. I squint, shade my eye against the glare of the low-hanging sun. The figure is a statue of Neptune, muscular and sensuous, crafted with impeccable skill. My heart skips a beat, then another. Arousal and dread wreak havoc within my stomach. One look at Reginald confirms that he finds himself in a similar state, as if there's something in the air that our bodies react to. I watch him absentmindedly touching himself, then cast around for something ...

Reginald points at a small hill, fifteen yards to our right.

"Come on, this is going to be special."

I hesitate for a moment, waiting for my heartbeat to settle, then follow him as he half-walks, half-runs to the hill, and disappears from sight.

***

Incongruously, the hill hides an antique, spiral stairwell. The entrance gate's padlock lies in pieces on the floor. Damp, mildewy air emanates from inside, carrying hints of rotting wood, decaying stones. I can hear water drip, drip, drip below, the sound echoing off green-tiled walls. My heart palpitates wildly, my arousal — almost painful now — waxes and wanes between the heart flutters. I stand motionless. Inexplicable dread prevents me from entering the stairwell.

"Emrys, I need you." Reginald's muffled voice like a beacon in a storm. It calms me, gives me direction, brings me back to myself.

The green tiles remind me of some of the older underground tunnels in London. That same combination of craftsmanship and industrial endeavour is replicated here. There's a beauty to the tiles, even with their glazing cracked in a hundred places, causing thousands of jagged lines to web across the formerly smooth surfaces.

I count exactly ninety-nine steps down to the bottom of the stairwell. Each step swallows more of the day's light, until I arrive in almost complete darkness to stand next to Reginald. We're in a tunnel, a slight breeze jostles Reginald's generous, curly locks. Even clothed in gloom he remains beautiful.

The tunnel runs in two directions. One leads into terrible, thick darkness, the other to a sickly, yellow glow, dancing erratically in the gloom.

"Which way?" I whisper the words.

"To the light. The other way connects with the old estate. There's a door, it's locked. I already checked."

"What if somebody comes?" I stare into the cloying dark until I see the faintest outline of a heavy door.

"The estate burned down a few years ago. I don't think there's any guards. Just fences and alarms."

We start moving, slowly at first, until we gain some night vision and with it a measure of confidence. Details emerge: slimy limescale stalactites patiently drip water into the tunnel. Not enough to cause problems, but creating some slippery patches and giving colonies of subterranean, wet moss a foothold into this world. Some of the growth seems to exhibit faint bioluminescence. I don't understand how this can be. Slugs drag themselves across the green tiles, layering intersecting trails of fresh slime across old, dried-up spoors. I notice an outsized beetle ponderously chewing a piece of meat of unknown origin.

The ground is driest in the middle of the tunnel, with only minor puddles accruing where the tiled walls and floor meet. The smell of rot and mildew is more pervasive now, with added hints of iron, like at a butcher's shop.

The echo of our footsteps competes with the irregular dripping and splashing sounds that pervades the air.

The tunnel curves to the left, opens up unto a surreal tableau:

We stand in a circular ballroom, no less than twenty yards across. Bearing down on us; a curved, glass and metal dome. At the apex, perhaps forty feet high, stands Neptune, leering at us through the water of the lake, his trident aimed at the heart of the ballroom. We are completely submerged, buried under opaque, murky water.

The glass panels in the ceiling dome have turned a sickly yellow and green colour with algae and dirt, interspersed with random patches of red and blue — as if to break up the monotony of the light. The gently rippling waves on the surface and the low hanging sun — nothing more than an undulating blob in a smear of a sky — conspire to throw an extraordinary light-show across the ballroom, illuminating a scene rich with uncanny detail.

An optical illusion causes the black and white tiles of the square, central dance-floor to move in a confusing, rippling pattern. I feel sick and try to look away from the mesmerising but nauseating display. Curved benches, upholstered with brash, red velour, line the ballroom's walls. Delicate side tables, carried by wooden legs carved to resemble animal legs, are haphazardly spread around, as if they walked there out of curiosity, or boredom. Some have clustered together in a group, huddling in fear. A few still support tall, crystal glasses — their content evaporated decades ago, leaving behind a poisonous looking residue.

"My lovely Duchess told me that constructing all this took years, but that wasn't the real reason for the animosity towards the old lady and her lover."

Reginald's voice feels too sharp, as if he's trying to put on a brave face when he should whisper instead. It's his instinct to play to the audience, even if it's an audience of one.

I notice an exquisitely decorated, foldable room divider on the far side of the ballroom. In response, a sharp pain pulses, snakes, from my stomach to the base of my skull. I gasp audibly.

Oblivious, Reginald carries on; "The real trouble began after they finished this place, and the artificial lake was filled with water, and they started to make use of the ballroom—"

I feel myself move towards the room divider.

"—At first they threw typical high-society parties. Exclusive affairs, wowing elite guests with this amazing structure—"

There is something about the room divider screen I recognise ... The decorations are familiar to me. Figurines, abstracted people, hollow-eyed dancers ... it is becoming hard to concentrate.

"—But, the parties soon turned into something more ... risqué, shall we say? Whispers about carnal rituals started to circulate. Local youths were implicated ... Scandalous stories and rumours, all a bit too close to home for those in power—"

I push the room divider aside and find a large, ornate, metal clothes rack. A heavy, brass pole spans across; I can barely make out a collection of old-fashioned, lumpy costumes, hanging in quiet suspension.

"—So, when the local *noblesse obliges* finally decided that enough was enough, it didn't take long for the young entrepreneur to face drummed up charges of massive fraud. He was convicted soon after—"

I am drawn in to the costume rack. Its image threatens to dislodge something inside me. I want to know what it means. My legs move as if against a powerful stream, but I slowly advance. I see a dress I recognise. If I can only—

A hand touches my shoulder, spins me around. I'm too weak to resist. Reginald points at the glass dome above. There is movement, sickly grey and yellow flesh, lips soundlessly nibbling the glass, the slimy strands of vegetation, each other ... Lidless eyes catch the glow of the dying sun.

"That's amazing. They must think it's feeding time ..." Reginald's sharp voice brings the scene into focus. Giant carp ponderously swim around the dome, their bellies fat and the colour of dead flesh. Snake-like, dead-eyed eels, slither over each other, picking at invisible morsels and nuggets of debris floating in the water.

I am violently sick.

"Emrys, what on Earth? What's the matter with you?"

"We have to go. Now!"

"What do you mean? We have to set up my gear, photograph—"

"Shut up! Listen!"

Sound is a void, I'm barely aware of my own breathing. Then; metal scraping over metal. Rattling, a muffled voice.

I grab Reginald's hand. "The door!"

We run. Finally I surrender to the dread building inside me. I run from the thing that threatens to erupt in my mind. I run from the unnamed visitor, poised to enter the tunnel ahead of us.

As we flee the ballroom, the fish in the watery sky above us go into a frenzy — giant carp mouths silently gaping and snapping, eels contorting, squirming. Racing down the corridor I can hear music from behind us.

And finally, as we ascend the stairwell, I can hear soft laughter.

***

My loft is a cocoon, a womb, a shelter, yet it offers no protection from that which has already entered.

I draw, furiously, using whatever materials I can find. Charcoal, pen, pencil, ink. Every sketch book, every piece of parchment, every sheet of high-priced artisan pressed vellum, is filled with things I cannot suppress. Gaping fish heads, sloppily worn by human torsos. Mannequin arms ending in ruined stumps. Hollow eye sockets inside grotesque costumes, swerving erratically across a malformed ballroom dance floor.

I cover the walls with these things, as if they are clues in a bizarre crime drama. Maybe they are, but if that's the case I cannot for the life of me figure out the crime.

My landlady utters inanities at me through my locked door. *Worried about my health*, she says. Something about bringing me some *hearty, home-made chicken soup*. She knows about my CIPA affliction and has been trying to mother me ever since I told her, which I regret doing to this day. I play along and pretend to be grateful, accepting her stinking brew. Whatever ails me can't be cured by her. I know what I should do, but I simply can't bring myself to do it.

Reginald tries to ring me, but I hang up. He rings back, I disconnect the phone. Finally, I exhaust myself through sketching and drawing long enough to find a moment of calm, and attempt to clear my mind.

It is the wrong thing to do. Impossible questions bubble up, threatening me with answers I don't want to hear. *Why were the room divider decorations familiar to me? Who did the fish expect? Who else would visit the ballroom under the lake? Did I really hear laughter?*

I remember I still have an unopened bottle of Scotch in my larder, a present from Reginald to make up for one of his frequent insults. I don't remember the details of his indiscretion, but gratefully uncork the (no-doubt priceless) whiskey and imbibe greedy gulps, straight from the neck, like a tramp.

***

I play this charade for three days, hiding myself away from everything and everyone, but unable to hide from what is inside me and what I must do.

On the fourth day I finally ring Reginald. He agrees to meet with me.

This time I venture outside of my loft apartment to visit him. The world outside is too bright, too loud. I feel clumsy and ungraceful, like I don't belong out here. The people in the streets move with enviable fluidity, with a sense of life that clearly connects them to each other. How can I possibly fit in?

I arrive at Reginald's house. He's waiting outside by his car, equipment packed. I have never seen him like this; nervous, haggard, uncertain.

"You feel it too?" I ask.

"It's strong. I can't fight it anymore. We have to go back."

I nod. We embrace. At this moment I love him more than ever. We are the same. We are of a kind. He is the only person who can understand me — as am I to him — which creates a bond.

Like actors in a play, we enter his flashy little car and drive off towards the sunset, performing the role we are expected to play.

∗∗∗

Repeating the journey we made only four days ago, I'm overcome with a staggering sense of déjà vu, and an even stronger feeling of inevitability. Whatever will happen is unstoppable now. There's comfort in that.

"What happened to the entrepreneur?" I ask, trying to distract myself.

"What do you mean?"

"You said he was convicted of massive fraud ..."

"Yes ... it's extraordinary really. He knew what would happen I think, because on the day of sentencing he came prepared to end it."

"He brought a gun?"

"Cyanide pill. He killed himself right there in the chambers. His classy wife witnessed it all, had to be taken away to a mental home afterwards."

We return to the carriage house exactly at sunset. From a lurid red and purple sky, burning spears of light thrust through the structure's damaged roof. We rush down the desiccated mud path to the lake. We arrive just as the sun is swallowed by the water. I think of the creatures beneath and shudder. I want to go home, return to the womb of my loft apartment, instead I enter the orifice in the hill, descend the ninety-nine steps and wait for Reginald to join me in the tunnel. When he does, he blinds me with a wildly swinging torch.

"What are you doing?" I hiss, but understand his intent a moment later when Reginald walks not to the ballroom, but to the door at the other end of the tunnel. I follow.

The torch reveals a heavy, wooden door with rusted hinges, lock and bolts. The handle squeaks as Reginald pushes down on it. The door won't budge. He tries to push the bolts across in the locked position, and although there is some movement, he can't finish the job.

"Help me, come on."

We both push, and to my surprise, with a grinding and screeching sound the bolts slide into place.

"That's better," pants Reginald, looking smug. I'm not reassured.

I take a breath, gather courage, and set off towards the ballroom. The air in the tunnel feels different; not so cold, or humid, although the sense of decay and rot is still there, grabbing at me like a physical force. The cracked, green subway tiles around me remind me of being squeezed by a giant snake. I rush out of the tunnel to get away from its oppressive embrace.

The ballroom is as we found it last time. Once again, the sickly sunset light falls through the dome's glass panels, to animate the floor, the walls, the sofas. The decrepit drinks remain as ghosts of ancient parties. The tables on animal legs have not changed position. Nonetheless something is different somehow; I can feel it. I look up, find the water free of fish. This time our audience is just the two of us.

"What was it for you?" I ask Reginald. I know he understands the question.

"The dance floor," he mumbles. "I can see myself ... I can't explain it." Reginald, lacking in courage as ever, sticks to the walls, dragging his index finger across the fitted sofas, the coffee tables, the glass panels of the magnificent dome. It squeaks softly as his flesh moves across the cold glass surface.

I can smell the change before I see it. Sandalwood and Linseed oil.

Then, a hint of music. *Duke Ellington? Count Basie?* Something to dance to.

I finally face the twisted, decorated room divider. Uncanny shapes expertly painted and grafted into the old wood beckon me forwards. Pressure builds up inside me. The music rises in volume. Reginald groans.

As before I am drawn towards the clothing frame beyond the divider. This time I'll discover its meaning, I'm sure of it.

The ambient light changes, brightening the room. More detail of the ballroom's luxurious content manifests all around me. The exquisite carving of the animalistic table legs, the elegant, precise curves of the velour sofas; its upholstery in perfect condition and outrageously red. Even the minute facets in the crystal drinks glasses; no longer empty but sparkling with bubbling champagne and shocking green absinthe. I look up at the dirty, decaying dome, and find it restored to a pristine state. I can see bright clouds, a fresh blue sky, the rippling lake surface barely a barrier against a glorious midday sun.

I can hear Reginald whimper, but my eyes are firmly fixed to what lies beyond the divider. The metal clothes rack, its brass pole, the lumpy costumes hanging beneath. The music swells in volume.

The light changes again, golden beams spearing the gloom around the clothes rack. The strange costumes finally reveal themselves to be occupied by life-sized wooden dolls, with painted heads that hang at wrong angles and feature simple, articulated joints, blunt torsos, tubular limbs. They remind me of theatrical dolls, with large, white-painted holes for eyes and over-sized clunky hands and feet. They all wear different costumes, different expressions. Anger, mirth, sly evil. A sickening, unexplainable familiarity with this scene draws me closer.

I can sense her presence just when my memories come flooding back to me like stale bilge, trapped inside an abandoned vessel for too many years, finally released through a calamitous hull breach.

I turn around slowly, barely able to move. She holds Reginald prone by single-handedly grabbing his curly hair with immense strength.

Reginald can't escape, his body is motionless save for some involuntary jerking and twitches.

She wears her red party dress, her black gloves, her sturdy, silver pumps. Her husky voice rasps with age and lust. "What did you bring me this time Reginald? Your little bout of wanderlust was satisfying I hope?" Her mouth opens impossibly wide and I cry a single tear as her teeth scrape across Reginald's hardening forehead. She feeds like a glutton; sucking, chewing, extracting Reginald's experiences of the last few years, and she transforms both of them in the process. When she's done, she lazily dances with him, dragging his stiff limbs across the ballroom floor with swaying, sensuous moves. I can't help but respond with shameful arousal. The dance seems to go on for an eternity but eventually the song stops, and she drops Reginald to the floor. His beautiful, ebony-skinned face, his wonderful, intricate curls, the intelligent mouth; reduced to a grotesque wooden caricature with large, dumb, empty eyes and a horrifically racist set of painted red lips.

"And you Emrys? What have you brought home to me?"

I fall to the floor. My head bounces once before it lies still. There is no pain.

She takes more time with me, having already sated herself partially on Reginald's collected experiences. She returns to her meal several times before her body is restored again, her skin smooth, her curves filled out. I don't get the benefit of a dance.

"Would you like to be reunited with Judith?"

Her long-nailed, perfectly manicured index and middle finger enter my empty eye-sockets and she drags me across the floor. I am blind while her claws reside in the painted wooden hollows but I know where she takes me. A jolt at my neck where the hanger is placed, a rough upward jerk, and I hang next to her other victims on the metal rack. This is where I will reside, awaiting her pleasure, or — in a decade or two — the rare, coveted price of a brief period of existence outside, where we sometimes are sent to live our little fake lives; dutiful puppets performing for our lady.

My badly hinged, ill-fitting jaw clacks feebly as I attempt to scream.

BIOGRAPHY

Rudolf is a BAFTA nominated veteran game developer, author, photographer, producer, father, husband, cat person, filmmaker, dog person, and consultant. (Not necessarily in that order). Originally of Dutch/Spanish descent, he currently lives and works as an interactive entertainment consultant in Canterbury.

He has worked with clients across the entertainment landscape for more than 22 years, including companies like Lionsgate Studios, Framestore and Electronic Arts, providing design and consultancy work for some of the biggest intellectual properties in the world.

Rudolf has written a textbook on game design (published by CRC Press), a gaggle of short stories, two novels, several screenplays, and an abundance of video game narratives.

He continues to write short-and-longform sci-fi, horror, weird fiction, historical fiction, non-fiction, and whatever other genre or muse he succumbs to, and plans to do so until the sun dims, or his time on Earth passes. (Whichever comes first!)

DEMAIN PUBLISHING

To keep up to-date on all news DEMAIN (including future submission calls and releases) you can follow us in a number of ways:

BLOG:
www.demainpublishingblog.weebly.com

TWITTER:
@DemainPubUk

FACEBOOK PAGE:
Demain Publishing

INSTAGRAM:
demainpublishing

Printed in Great Britain
by Amazon